BROKEN WINGS AND BURIED SECRETS

BETHANY VOTAW

For Malachi

BUTTONS

"What are you doing here, Jackie?" Granny asked, a smile plastered on her face. "Oh, Linda is here too!"

"Hi Granny." I trudged up the few steps of her front porch. It felt like climbing a mountain. "Mom and I came by to say hi—right, Mom?" I glared at my mother, clenching the handle of my small suitcase a little too tightly.

"Way to let me do the talking," she mumbled. My mom turned to Granny. "Jackie is actually going to stay here for a few weeks while we look for someone more full-time."

"Oh?" Granny shuffled into her ancient kitchen. The yellowed walls and worn tiles made my skin crawl, but I couldn't help but smile when my eyes made their way to the familiar steam stain on the wall. She must have followed my eyes to the stove and because she put the kettle on.

Mom sat at the kitchen table and fiddled with the puzzle pieces sprawled across the surface.

"I've been working on that for weeks," Granny said, picking up a piece and putting it back down.

I stood, still clutching the suitcase. "So, should I take this to the spare room?"

"Yes." Mom flicked her hand away and started relaying the same information to Granny for the hundredth time. I made my way to the spare room, paused long enough to toss the suitcase on the bed, and shuffled to the back door, cigarette lit before I made it completely outside.

What the hell am I doing here?

Mom's voice jumped up an octave, the way it always did when talking to Granny. "You need some help here, remember? Jackie said she'd stay with you and help out for a bit. You haven't seen her for quite a while, either. She'll help you make food, do your washing and stuff... You'd like that."

"I am doing fine by myself," said Granny.

"I know," Mom said, "but if you want to stay here, you need some extra help. That or the home."

Granny mumbled something. Mom countered with, "Honestly, Jackie needs a place to lay low for a while. She's fresh out of treatment and needs some form of responsibility I know she can handle and to keep her occupied. She's always had a special connection with you."

I blew out a puff of smoke and pretended it was something else escaping my lungs. I couldn't help but grin when Mom screeched my name. After stomping the embers out, I made my way back in. "What's up?"

Mom pursed her lips and wore her signature underbite, turning to Granny. "Mom, I think your water is ready." When Granny turned, my mother led me from the kitchen in an iron grip. "What the hell are you thinking?"

I shrugged.

"Don't act like that. Jackie, for Christ's sake, you're twenty-seven years old! Act like it! This is seriously your last chance. Honest to God. *Last. Chance.*"

She was screaming, but in a whisper—a standing oxymoron. Then again, I was the one standing in this creaking house with a woman I'd have to babysit until my penance was paid. So really, I was the moron here.

"I mean it, Jackie. You're clean, right?"

I nod, my last shred of dignity stripped away.

"Good, now keep it up, but you steal—"

"*Borrow.*"

"Don't pull that with me. You steal *anything*, you're done. You decide to borrow her checkbook? Done. Take her car for a solo spin? Done. I mean it. Get your shit together. Use this time to reflect—plan something. Anything."

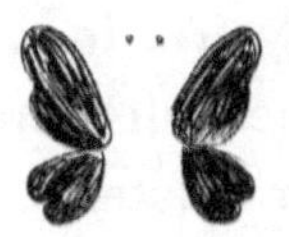

The first few days were fine. Granny seemed competent and normal. Still, she forgot to lock the doors and forgot she had put the kettle on more than once. She hummed along to the screaming pot until I reminded her *what* was screaming.

Then the sleepwalking started. I had to sleep with my door open so I could listen for when she tried to escape. I took to turning on the lights so when she woke, she could make it back to her room. Once she'd gotten dressed and ready for the day, the screaming of the kettle woke me. She wouldn't believe me when I told her it was three a.m. I had to take her out onto the porch so she could feel the night before she settled back in her room.

"Mom," I whispered into the phone one morning. "She forgot my name; I think she knew who I was, but I can't be sure."

I knew this was going to happen—but this happened to *other* people. Not to Granny. But when it happened, I certainly didn't expect to feel like the old woman slapped me across the face when she lost my name. After a few times, that sharp pain turned into a thorn of irritation.

"I know," Mom said. "She has good weeks and bad weeks . . . Looks like you're in a valley. Just ride it out. Make sure she takes her pills and drinks enough water. I'm dropping off groceries later."

I met Granny at the kitchen table for our ritual of eggs, toast, and scalding tea.

"You remember how I taught you to play poker?" Granny asked.

"I don't think that was what you taught me. Maybe it was Mom."

"Oh, no! It was you! We used to play with buttons."

"*That* was poker?" I searched my memories. I guess it was. *Maybe?* It must have been some simplified version a kid would understand. "You want to play?" The words fell out of my mouth before I could stop them.

"I'll try to remember how we played." She was already standing and making her way to the overstuffed bookshelf, fiddling with a jar of buttons. She struggled with the lid, still trying to open it when she sat back down. I took the jar and gave it a small turn, leaving her with the job of opening the rest. It was how I treated my nephews, back when I was allowed to see them. They liked to think they could do it all.

"I don't think I remember how to play," she said.

"Neither do I," I confessed. I searched the folds of my brain. *Did we use a deck of cards? It was like poker. Why don't I remember cards being there?*

Granny started to laugh, then cackled.

"What?"

"You're doing what I do," she said through her laughter.

"What?"

"Trying to remember. It's the pits, isn't it?" She played with the buttons in the jar and threw one at me. It hit me in the cheek.

"What the hell was that for?" I rubbed my face and looked around for where the button rolled.

"That was a memory. Poof! Gone!" She laughed. "Maybe we played like this." She used the edge of one to press it against a button on the table. The pressure became too much, and the white button went flying across the room.

"Poof," I whispered.

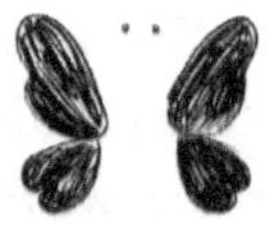

"What the hell, Mom?" My stomach knotted. It was only days after the button debacle, and she stood on the front lawn with two cops at her side.

"I meant it, Jackie," she said. Any pity or sadness she once held for me was clearly replaced by repulsion.

All she saw was a pile of shit. I couldn't blame her—I felt lower than dog shit—but I bit my tongue and spat, "What are you talking about?"

Of course, I knew exactly what this was about. Sort of. It was a matter of what sin she had come to collect a debt on. Then she held up a plastic bag with a pink floral check inside. My stomach dropped. She must have seen the look on my face.

"I told you," she seethed, "no more chances."

"Mom, I didn't steal it, forge it, nothing. Granny *gave* it to me."

"Don't blame her! You and I both know she needs coaching to make it through writing a check these days."

The tall and unassuming cop looked tired of the drama and stepped forward. "Jackie Olson?"

"Yeah." I hoped maybe a quiver would make it into my voice—make it sting a little for Mom—but instead, my voice was woody and resigned. As close to an admission of guilt as I'd come.

Then he started the Miranda Rights. I listened carefully, wishing I had my phone out to record; maybe he'd slip up and I'd get out on some technicality. But he didn't slip up. *Wait, what was I being arrested for? What did he say? Falsifying a check? Damn, I wish I had my phone.*

"What are you doing?" Granny shuffled onto the porch, two cups of tea in her hand. She made it down the two steps to the front yard. The cops ignored me while I took three involuntary steps toward her. These stairs were an obstacle when she had her hands free, but with her hands full of cups, I expected her to go ass over tea kettle.

When she made it down, she chuckled at the look of concern on my face. "Bet you thought I was going ass over tea kettle, huh?"

"I was thinking the same thing." I smiled; it was always funny hearing her say *ass*. "I've been spending too much time with you."

She handed me the steaming tea. Well, steaming *water*—she forgot to add a tea bag. Again. I cupped it in my slightly trembling hands and followed her to Mom and the cops.

"What is going on, Linda?" Granny's lips were pursed in a fine line, mirroring the look on my mother's face. I caught myself pressing my own lips together.

"Mom," my own mom started, "you know Jackie has had some problems. She was supposed to hang out with you for a few weeks to get settled and back on her feet. But she stole from you." She shook the plastic bag containing what looked like a singular check. "Look. She *stole* from you."

Granny's weathered hand reached out and took the bag and pulled it close to her face and squinted at it. "I wrote this check."

My stomach did a flip.

"What? You did?" Mom asked.

"I wrote it." Granny pointed at the evidence bag. "See? My signature and everything."

"Why on earth would you write a check for five hundred dollars, and where did you find your checkbook? I've had it with me, so you didn't lose it."

"I always keep a few in my billfold," she said. "Everyone should."

That much was true, but the rest were gone now. The other check burned a hole in my own wallet now, waiting for my pen to write Granny's name. Another five hundred waiting to be cashed.

"Did she ask you to write it?" Mom's expression was a perfect cocktail of repulsion and hope.

"Of course not! You raised a polite lady." Granny looked at her tea. Well, water. "I need a tea bag."

"Mom, why did you write her a check?"

"We were talking about life and school and whatnot."

Did we? What have we done these past days? Walked and talked. She watched me put together the puzzle, her only contribution picking up and setting down pieces. But she looked so happy when we finished. We went to the store and picked up the glue and I helped her paint it on a cardboard piece and we hung it up. What else did we do?

"She's gonna use that money to buy herself a computer. Nothing fancy—just one where she can register for classes and whatnot."

"She has one."

"No, she doesn't."

I did once—but I sold it to pay back some debts, ones I had conveniently forgotten about. But how would Granny know that?

Mom raised an eyebrow at me.

"Officers," Granny began, speaking so sweetly it was almost cliché, but the officers straightened at her syrupy voice. "I think there was a mistake here. I wrote that check for my granddaughter."

"Ma'am," the officer said, "if you do not want to press charges, there is nothing we can do." He looked at my mom. "I think we'll be on our way." He tipped his hat to us as if he were a cowboy bidding good day to a gaggle of girls. I wanted to flip him the bird but managed to hold the cup of hot water and give him a polite nod back.

Granny was halfway to the porch by the time Mom and I caught up with her.

"I think I left the kettle on," she muttered. I trailed behind, prepared for her to teeter over, but I'd be there to catch her.

When we sat back at the kitchen table, I turned the

kettle on (it was off, despite Granny's insistence she had left it on).

"So." Mom cleared her throat. "What classes are you thinking about?"

No apologies, no admission of wrongdoing. Par for the course. But then again, I'm the same way.

I frantically searched my brain, looking for something to say, to sound competent, like I had a plan despite acting like a bird and burying my head in the sand. Granny grinned at me from across the table.

Memory fading, my ass. She hadn't lost that sweet Granny style of manipulation. She enjoyed this. Did she just wink?

"Well." I stood and fetched the hot water. It was barely warm, but I needed the spare moment to think. I spent my time figuring out what tea I wanted, though I picked the one I always reached for and made my way back to the table where the two ever-patient women sat. "I was planning on registering for some classes at the community college." It seemed like the answer they would approve of. "And I was thinking of just getting those Mickey Mouse classes over with, you know, like the general math and English crap."

Mom nodded. "Okay, okay, that's good. Any ideas about what else you are planning?"

Isn't it enough that I am looking into the future? Why do I need a five-year plan?

Granny read my mind. "I think it's a swell plan. Didn't you mention something about math?"

"Yeah." *Did I say that?* "But I want to keep my options open."

"Not *too* open, I hope," Mom said. She turned to Granny. "You didn't have to do that."

"'Course, I did! How else was she gonna get all registered and stuff?"

Mom shook her head and checked her watch. "Got to run; I'll swing by later with groceries." And she fled. I wanted to run away too. Leave this house, the memories, or lack of them.

Granny snickered and sipped her now room-temperature water.

"Thanks," I mumbled.

"It is a gift." She smiled. "Now do something with it."

"That's very Jean Valjean of you," I said.

"I think I know him. We go to church together."

I thought she was joking, but I couldn't be sure. "Thanks," I said, and I felt myself wracking my brain for what courses I'd take.

The nights got worse. She was up at all hours, wandering. I caught her rearranging her bookshelves again; she didn't seem startled by me being in her house, despite her not remembering who I was. I liked to think she had my face wobbling around in her brain and she was aware that she knew me, like a word on the tip of her tongue. I still couldn't remember how we played poker with buttons; the jar still sat on the table, laughing at me.

"Have some tea with me," she said—chipper, as always.

Tea? I raced to the kitchen to discover an empty pot and a stovetop glowing red. She'd have set the house on fire. Still, I filled the kettle and set it back on the glowing stove. When it whistled, we took our usual seats at the table.

She nodded at nothing, sipping slowly. "What do you think dying will be like?"

I nearly choked. *Maybe like this.* "You feeling okay, Granny? Do I need to take you to the hospital?"

"No, no. I am fine. But I think I have died." She poured the jar of buttons onto the table. "What do you do when part of you dies?"

"I don't know, Granny."

She scooped up a handful of the buttons and dropped them on the table; the small clanking of each button slapping the surface made me jump.

"Poof," she said.

"Poof." I nodded.

"I can't be sad, because I don't remember what I forget. But I know I forget." She let out a long sigh through a small smile. "But then I talk, and I can't tell if I am talking about things that happened or things I thought of or dreams or anything in between."

I could relate to that. I started classes the following week, concentrating in math. Did we talk about that? Was that a dream? What did I forget, and why did the idea of forgetting make me feel worse than remembering all the bad?

There was nothing to say, so we spent the early hours

of the morning playing with the buttons, snapping them across the table, dropping them from our hands, listening to their clunking and clicking. But this time, I didn't put them back in the jar when we were finished.

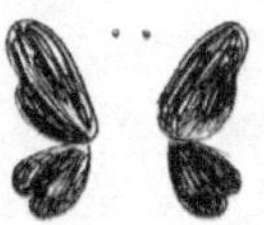

Mom helped me pack up the boxes—they would be stored in her attic and garage until they decided to sell or rent the house. I kept some books, that blasted jar of buttons too.

"I just want to clear out this place," Mom said. She was a doer, always had been.

"Doesn't feel like home anymore," I said. She hugged me, fierce and tight and it felt raw and real.

We made tea, but it didn't taste the same.

"She was proud of you," Mom said.

My throat tightened. I swallowed the hot liquid, the burn welcome. "She was proud of all her kids and grandkids."

"You were special to her, though." Mom cleared her throat too. "She left you this." Mom pulled out a stack of checks wrapped tightly with a rubber band from her purse. They were that gaudy pink. Mom cleared her throat again. "She had me help get your school stuff figured out. Each check here should pay for a semester."

My throat constricted again, so tight I couldn't breathe. "She did that?"

"She told me I could hang on to them, you know . . ."

Of course, I know.

"But whenever you start a new semester, it's here. Just—"

"I know," I interrupted, the pressure behind my throat was too much. "Don't mess it up."

"Just do your best, honey."

I tried to keep the tears at bay when we locked up the house and descended the steps we'd taken so many times before. It was weird leaving, knowing that I didn't have a reason to come back to this house.

Mom and I pretended not to notice each other's tears on the drive to the funeral. The best and worst thing of my year. All my family—the little nephews, too—all in one place. We took turns walking to that open casket. Some whispered a few words. Others dropped in notes and photos.

When it was my turn, I shuffled forward. "You finally went ass over tea kettle," I whispered, and I flipped a button into her casket. A gaudy pink one.

PAY TO THE
ORDER OF   Jackie
Five Hundred and
College
FOR
012345678
1001001234
0123
PAY TO THE
ORDER OF   Jackie
Five Hundred and
College
FOR   345678
1001001234
0123

BROKEN WINGS

At first, the girl tried to use coat hangers—the broken ones shoved in the back of the closet. But Mama found out and took them away, scolding her for taking what wasn't hers. Then Mama tossed the mangled wire hangers into the dark corners of the cupboard.

The girl was tempted to go after them—the sting on her backside was not enough to warn her off this time. So she used the old chicken wire she found lying in the barn. She bent and twisted the wire just so and created oblong and uneven wings. She wrapped plastic grocery bags from the supermarkets around them. White would have to do. The shoddy product made her smile. The straps were made from old hay twine and she pulled the wings over her shoulders, like a backpack of sorts.

She had to dodge her papa, though—he was home all the time now 'cause work didn't want him no more. He drank all the bottles in the house and slept in the barn with the pigs. That's what Mama called him. *A pig.* "Go make a bed with your own kind," she said.

"These should do!" the girl proclaimed, jumping from puddle to puddle when she was out of her papa's reach. The wings bounced against her back as she ran. It seemed like she jumped higher when she wore the wings. The girl thought she may even get stuck in the clouds. She only paused a moment before she decided to try.

"They won't miss me," the girl told herself, looking at the sky. The kids in her favorite books always said that when they wanted to run away. It was the truth, though. It was permission.

So she clambered atop that bridge that led into town and let her eyes focus on the perfect, fluffiest cloud. She flew. And she was right—they didn't miss her.

It took years for them to find that plastic-covered, bent-up chicken wire tangled at the bottom of the river.

THANK YOU, LORD

"Davie," Grandma said with her tight lips and high voice. "Fold your hands, close your eyes, and say your prayer."

It sounded like a request, but little Davie knew a command when he heard one. He cast a quick glance at his dad, who was sitting across the table. He was already bowing in supplication to the lasagna, or God, or Grandma, or whatever.

Davie closed his eyes for only a moment before they snapped open again, staring at the steam rising from the dish of fresh lasagna. How could Grandma expect a prayer when faced with melting cheese and the smell of garlic bread? Especially after a long morning at the church place.

". . . and we all say amen," Grandma finished.

Davie wasted no time and dove right in, taking a giant bite of the gooey cheese. It burned the roof of his mouth. He must have flinched because Grandma gave him a rather satisfied look. His punishment for not praying right was the pain, but the taste of melted cheese and meat sauce felt much better than the burn.

He swallowed the steaming lasagna and took a bite from the garlic bread, chewing loudly. *That will show her.* The burn was worth the bite, it always was.

Grandma dabbed at her thin lips, careful to fix her lipstick lines between each bite with the napkin. They had never used napkins at home before, but when she came to live with them, she *insisted* each person have one—for each meal, too. Davie used his sleeve, anyway.

Grandma should be less selfish, Davie thought. She'd already dragged them to church that morning. Making them use napkins, too? It was just too much.

"Why do we have to go?" Davie had asked his father that morning.

"Because Grandma asked us too" was as close of an answer as Davie got. His father turned the conversation into another "when I was a boy your age" story. Davie stopped listening. He was good at turning off his ears like that.

He stopped listening in church too. He was sandwiched between Dad and Grandma and the words from the man up front turned into a blended blur of nothing, like a fly buzzing in his ear.

Church was a sad time because it was a slow time. Nothing to do with his hands, his mind, his body. Nothing to do but listen to the fly-preacher guy buzz in his ear and think. And he always thought of Grandpa. Grandpa taught him how to spit right, how to wink, and how to cast a good fishing line. Grandpa taught him how to *pray right.*

The right way to pray always started with a "Thank you, Lord." *Thank you, Lords* should come after each meal when the belly is full, and after you catch a giant trout, or when you make it to supper just on time. *Thank you, Lords* went like, "Thank you, Lord, for this melted cheese," or "Thank you, Lord, for the cold river to swim in."

After each day out with Grandpa, Davie would say, "Thank you, Lord, for Grandpa."

And Grandpa used to say, "Thank you, Lord, for my Davie boy."

Grandpa used to give the best hugs, a full body squeeze that smelled of peppermint and tobacco. He would never let go first, only when Davie was ready. Sometimes Davie was ready in a second, especially when they needed to get another cast out before dinner time. Sometimes it took him several minutes to master his tears and finally let go.

Grandma did not hug right. She'd pinch and grab, and Davie suffocated in her syrupy rose smell. It was a game of tug-of-war, and not the fun kind. Even now, as Davie cleared his plate and begged to go outside, he was stuck in Grandma's arms. She tried to wipe the lasagna from his mouth with her lipstick-stained napkin, but he broke free. Aas the screen door slammed shut behind him, he whooped and hollered, "Thank you, Lord!"

LIAR, LIAR

He couldn't be certain when it all started. Perhaps just before Christmas, when Mom and Dad went for each other's throats and promised to work through it again in January. Mrs. Shelly said it was wrong to blame them for things. She didn't understand, though. January was like that—the keeper of promises expected to be broken. January seemed like an acceptable point in time to blame.

He supposed it all *really* began when his stories grew too close to reality. At first, no one cared. One time he told Jane that her older sister had been stealing all her good pens and he got to watch them fight it out in the parking lot after school. He told Aaron that Mary liked him. And he told Mary that Aaron liked her. Then he got to watch them act strange around each other. He told Jeremy that Wilson stole his dessert from his lunch pail and got to watch them bloody each other up, all while he licked the crumbs from his own lips. It was all good fun. And then it wasn't.

He told the kids at lunch how he managed to stop a pack of coyotes from attacking Mrs. Gardner's chihuahua. "They were circling him, in his yard. I dunno where Mrs. Gardner was, probably inside, couldn't hear their yipping and barking over the TV." He told them how he charged into the pack of coyotes with just a fistful of rocks and yelled, "Get out!" with his deepest voice. He puffed out his chest and demonstrated, and Heather was so impressed she touched his arm and held his hand. She might have even kissed him too if there weren't so many people around. She was shy like that.

But his mom got to him. Someone told and she made him tell her the whole story. So he did. "You're lying to me," she said.

"No, I'm not!" he said.

"You bite your lip when you finish with your lie. Just for a second. But I notice. Now tell me the truth."

And so he did. And he knew he couldn't trust his parents again.

But he continued to tell stories, to lie. He told his mom about joining the math club, returning wallets to the police station, and other stories like that. It was better than them finding out what he really did for fun.

And when summer came, he was caught by Jane's older sister. He'd been sneaking into her underwear drawer. He had to lie again. It was embarrassing, but it was better to tell his mom he wanted to touch her panties than the truth—that Jane's older sister hid her pot in there and it was just too easy to get. Lying to his mom was easier than telling her that he'd been stealing bits of her stash for months, that he and the other kids would ride their bikes to the abandoned barn on the edge of town, where they'd smoke pot and drink whatever else they found. But he bit his lip when he told his mom about the panties, and she knew he was lying.

She sent him to a specialist, a child psychologist. Just the dumbed down, second-rate kind, since they couldn't afford a real one. Mrs. Shelly. The school counselor or something like that. He lied some more, talking about weird sex stuff just so the other kids wouldn't get in trouble too. And soon the lies made her smile. *Progress*, she called it.

The boy continued telling his lies and spinning his stories to keep his parents and Mrs. Shelly busy. Teachers too. Eventually, he stopped biting his lip. And on what was his last visit to Mrs. Shelly's office, she said she was happy with all the progress he'd made.

"Now what did you learn from all of this lying nonsense?" she asked him.

He looked her in the eye and told her, "I should trust adults and come to them when I have problems." He didn't bite his lip.

Mrs. Shelly smiled and said he didn't need to see her anymore, and that he'd finally figured out what it meant to be an adult.

BEES AND BEARS

Aunt Linnie said he needed to keep his eyes up, that it was much easier to see the world as a whole and make the right decisions. Bear always thought it was better to keep his eyes planted at the ground, looking for the sticks and stones people hurled at him so he wouldn't trip on those too.

"Just gotta pay those little gnats no mind," Aunt Linnie said from her spot on the sofa.

Aunt Linnie only had one leg. She lost the other due to *"die-of-beetus."* Bear thought it was rather lucky that it only killed her leg and not her whole self.

"Now go get a pack of peas and press it on that eye— it's already looking nice and purple, like a prune."

Bear nodded and trudged to the freezer. The pack of peas was more mush than anything else; it had been thawed and frozen and re-thawed so many times it was designated as Bear's personal ice pack.

"Don't forget now, keep your head up!" Aunt Linnie

hollered from her throne. "It'll be easier to see where the fists are coming from too."

People told Bear to live up to his name. To be big and brave and bold. Bear was the smallest in his glass of fifth graders. He always wore a sunburn and people pinched the freckles on his arms, asking, "When are they all gonna merge together and make you the right color?"

Bear didn't talk a lot. He knew how. Of course, he knew how. But he just chose to keep to himself, eyes down. Invisible, but not invisible enough. He was so pale and small he thought he might become transparent, see through, and really become nothing. His shock of red hair foiled that dream, though.

"Oh, Bear," Mrs. Tilde said. "Oh, it's not that bad. I knew Ruthie didn't mean to hit you that hard."

Bear bit his lip, his blue and purple eye throbbed with each step he took.

"Just your fair skin, dear, makes it look much worse than it really is."

Bear didn't say anything. He never did.

They were reading *Charlotte's Web*, and they each had to go around and say what character they wanted to be and why. All the girls said Charlotte. The boys said Wilbur, some said Templeton.

"And you, Bear? Which character do you want to be?"

He squared his eyes forward, looking at the whole room, just like he was supposed to. "I—I think I wanna be Fern." The class snickered. His eyes fell to the floor. "I just think it would be nice to live on a farm, and eat pancakes like her, you see?"

Mrs. Tilde chided the class but didn't press the matter. Bear supposed she was relieved the exchange was over too.

The bus rides were the worst. There were no teachers to save Bear. He was hunted just like out in the wild, except he had nowhere to run, no den to hide in. Not even a tree to climb.

"Bear, oh, Bear." Ruthie flicked the back of his ear. "You should eat those pancakes you talked about earlier —your little arms are just so cute, like a baby's. I could just snap them in half." She pinched his skin. It was like a bee sting.

"Oh, you know what I just thought of?" Ruthie jumped up from her seat and plopped down next to him. The eyes of the other kids followed her, and she smiled a wicked grin, like a hyena. Did hyenas chase bears? "I was just thinking that we could pinch your freckles together, make you that one color instead of the spotted cow." She pinched his arm again, turning any of the spaces between freckles red.

Bear didn't say anything, he never did.

When he finally got off the bus, he rubbed his arms, blaming the tears on his bruised eye. "Probably all hot and swollen," Aunt Linnie said from her usual spot. He hadn't seen her away from the couch in a long time. She ate there, slept there, folded laundry there.

It was the next morning that his Aunt Linnie noticed the bruises; the red had faded to pink, then overnight little blue dots appeared, like a blackberry bush coming to life on his arms.

Aunt Linnie bit her lip. "Get me one of the Cokes from the fridge."

Bear did as he was told. He held the cold glass bottle out to her.

"For you," she said.

He smiled wide. So did Aunt Linnie; her gap-toothed grin smelled like sugar. "Figured you needed a pick-me-up. Go on, now. Don't miss the bus!"

Bear shoved the bottle in his patched-up backpack and ran out to the bus which was already bouncing over the gravel road. It was that pothole-covered road that was his demise because as soon as the bus started forward again, the bouncing and jostling made the coke bottle emit its signature *clink!*

"Whatcha got there?" Ruthie asked. She assaulted the bag before Bear could say anything, not that he would have.

"Thank you, little Bear," she cooed. "I am *so* thirsty." She used the window's ledge to pop it open. She drank it down, the sweet sugary liquid dribbling down her chin; more spilled from the corner of her mouth with each bump of the bus.

Bear licked his lips, almost tasting the rare treat. Aunt Linnie would be sad—those were her special drinks. He wouldn't say anything, he never did.

But instead of going home on the bus, Bear decided to walk. He wondered if there were such things as lone bears. Lone wolf sounded cooler, but the idea was the same. See, he found a lollipop on the playground. A whole lollipop, wrapped and everything. Someone must have dropped it, and it was finders keepers. He wanted to enjoy it in peace.

The stick was thin and white like him, the candy had a red top, like him. *Cherry.*

Walking took a lot longer than the bus, but that sweet lolly was worth it. Eventually he made it on that bouncy gravel road; it was much better on foot. He was thankful that it was dry, that way his socks didn't get wet from the cracks in his soles. And he was left wondering if a soul could get cracks too, if that was a disease like "*die-of-beetus.*"

He paused when he got to Ruthie's house. The bus surely made it and dropped her off already. He had to make sure to sneak by. Maybe she was inside. He tossed the wrapper of the lolly aside, hiding the evidence of his own treat, just in case she frisked him for anything else.

He heard a hollering and yelling coming from the house. It wasn't Ruthie, though. It was a man, his words slurred and thunderous. He was throwing branches on a pile out pack, preparing to burn trash and debris.

Ruthie was out there with him, tossing twigs and broken fence pieces onto the growing pile. She wore the same dress on the shore at school today, stains from the Coke still on her front.

"Got a call from your teacher!" the man bellowed, bending low and slow to pick up a branch. He pointed it at Ruthie. "You're gonna get held back. You stupid girl."

Bear wondered if maybe she'd end up dying because of "*die-of-beatings.*"

The man threw the branch over the fire, and it smacked Ruthie in the arm. She didn't say anything. He picked up another. "You're a stupid girl." He threw it again, hitting her other shoulder.

She yelped, and he had her in his grip in only four strides. The resounding smack was like a gunshot at the racetrack, and Bear was gone, fleeing to Aunt Linnie's house. She sat on her couch and made him say "thank you" for the sweet treat he didn't have a chance to have that morning. Aunt Linnie liked being thanked, liked feeling useful.

The next morning when Ruthie sat in the seat next to him, she slugged his arm. "Didn't see you here yesterday, Bear boy."

Bear opened his mouth to speak, which must have surprised Ruthie. She sat back and waited, her own mouth open, waiting, ready to pounce and tear at whatever he was about to say with her teeth.

"Y-your dad hits you," Bear said.

She hit him, right in the same eye. A new layer of blue to add over the sick art she already created on his face.

Aunt Linnie didn't notice the new color.

But Ruthie was gone the next day.

And the day after that.

And the day after.

And finally, when enough kids were wondering where the queen bee was—funny how a bee was bigger than a bear—Mrs. Tilde told the class that Ruthie broke her arm. And collar bone. And maybe wrist.

Bear should have felt bigger then, and the bee was gone.

But the bear never felt smaller.

BURIED SECRETS

Mee-maw was the only one I could go to. She wasn't my first choice; she was never a first choice for anyone. But when my belly started to swell and the eviction notice came, it was her door I was knocking on. That walk up the long drive with my little valise and the little bump was worse than any other walk of shame I've trekked before.

"Put your bag in the back and start peelin' potatoes," she said. Her white hair was in a tight bun, the creases in her lips prominent after a lifetime of pursed lips. I did as she said. The room in the back was small—a bed and dresser, a small window too. *Could be worse*, I thought while staring at the little room. *I could be with my mother.*

"Get you and that belly out here! Quit dawdling!"

We peeled potatoes and she hummed a shaky song. "Quit sticking your belly out." I tried not to look offended, and Mee-maw quickly added, "It's bad for your back."

I stood straighter for the first time since the news five months ago. She scolded me for adding too much salt. I set the table and we sat across from each other.

"What's your plan?" she asked.

No warning, but that was fair—I had given her no warning either.

"Find a job, maybe wait until..." I patted the bump too hard and almost winced at myself. I wanted Mee-maw to know this was *not* what I wanted. I cleared my throat. "Wait until this is out and then find work. People aren't likely to hire me right now."

"What are you gonna do in the meantime?"

She knew the answer. Of course, she did. She just wanted to hear me say it. To humble myself in front of her. No point in prolonging the inevitable. "Figured I'd help you, until... you know, the baby is born." I caressed my swelling belly, and tried to make the word *baby* come across softly, but it was quite clear to the both of us that the affection was a farce.

"You're gonna pull your weight around here," she said, stuffing the potatoes in her mouth, chewing. "Just 'cause you're growing doesn't mean you get to slack off— it seems like you're in *that* position from that type of living, anyhow."

I shoved a potato down my throat and hoped it would get lodged there. Death by potato didn't seem that terrible of a way to leave this earth.

"I need help with the cows and such," Mee-maw said. "And the washing. Good Lord, I hate the washing. Tell you what, though—I know the widower down the road could use some help in that department too. He'd probably pay you a bit to do his laundry each week as well. You can keep it so long as you agree to do my washing too."

The idea of making anything at that point was intriguing. I nodded and mumbled a thank you. And that was it. She asked after Mama and confessed that she hadn't seen her in ages. I admitted that I hadn't either.

"What a fool of a woman," Mee-maw said. I was forced to agree; I was a carbon copy of her in everything but eye color. A moment later, she sighed, eyeing my belly. "Any idea who the daddy is?"

That stung—the assumption and accusation behind it was a slap in the face. I sat up straighter. "Yes, I do," I lied. She was right to assume I wouldn't know, but the story I was spinning in my head was a nice fantasy to live in. Too nice to let it go.

"He was a coal miner," I started, and that part had been true. I *had* been with a coal miner for a while—I cleaned the row houses, and got a little too familiar. It didn't last; his wife came home. So I made the ending different in my head. "We were gonna get married and live in one of those little row houses."

"Coal mining is a dangerous business," she said, the little wisps of her gray hair framing her face.

"I know," I spat. "He died." I was surprised by my own emotion. I suppose it was like he'd died to me. He was alive. But I mourned him for a day and got in with a carpenter the next town over. I started working as a cleaner there too. Maybe he was the father. Maybe he would have been a better story.

"I'm sorry," Mee-maw whispered, and I think she really meant it. She knew of love and loss, after all.

"It's all right. My own mistake, the whole milk before the cow thing," I said. And I felt like I reclaimed some respect then, if not a crumb of dignity. Maybe it was the old farmer's son, the one going all the way east for college... He would've been a good story too.

"Well, we'll get things straightened out," she said.

I almost believed her.

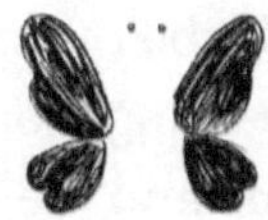

I hate cows. I hate their soupy shit, their sour smell, and I hate waking up at the crack of dawn to wade in that soupy shit and sour smell to play with their udders to try and milk one of those beasts. The belly got in my way too, but old Mee-maw proudly proclaimed she milked her cows up until the day she gave birth to my mama and only took that day off.

"I would have your mama sucking on one teat of mine while I worked on the teats of the cows."

I grimaced and nearly vomited. *This*—this was my last resort. A flutter in my stomach made me jump, and a kick made me grunt. It always made me grunt.

The weeks of bending over a washbasin and the early mornings had taken a toll on me. My eyes had new dark circles and my lips were cracked. Mee-maw looked good for however old she was or maybe she looked like shit for how young she was.

"Mee-maw!" I hollered over the cow and the sound of milk hitting the bucket.

"What is it?"

"How old are you?"

"None of your damn business."

I did the math—my mama was forty-two, and she must have been in her twenties. Mid-sixties then? I hated math. Part of me hoped this thing in me was a girl so I wouldn't have to fuss with all the schooling, and then a pang hit my heart and I wasn't sure why. Maybe I really did want a girl. Maybe I wanted this after all.

I found myself dreaming, sort of. I thought about Mama leaving her mama and me leaving mine. I started to enjoy the rhythm of milking and the grasshoppers chirping. Mee-maw hummed a song and spoke kindly to the cows. For a moment, I was a kid again, racing between the legs of the animals that once towered over me, gulping that warm cream while Mee-maw wasn't looking.

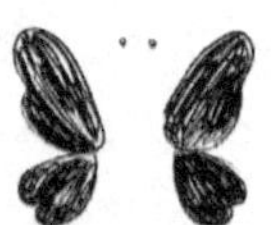

I was convinced my bladder was the size of a squirrel's. I had to waddle to the washroom three times every night—this dang kid just enjoyed sleeping right on top of it. The summer's moon was light enough for each trip, and the little treks through the kitchen had become a ritual. I prayed for something, maybe nothing, but I spoke the words all the same. I prayed that my mama was okay, that Mee-maw's old fingers would keep up with her life, and that the daddy wouldn't find me.

The last prayer always made the baby jump. I knew who it was. There was only one man it could've been, despite my hopping around. He and I had been together for a long while. I worked in the cereal factory he managed, and I'd sneak away to his house in the evenings, sometimes even midday.

He made me feel some special sort of way, and it went on for maybe more than a year. It'd been the most stable life I'd ever had.

The sight of cornbread left on the counter interrupted my running thoughts. Mee-maw never left cornbread out like this. She never made this much, either. The bread was cut into nice little servings, a saucer of butter right next to it. She knew how much I liked my butter.

I snacked on the bread and stared out the window, letting the crumbs fall onto my belly.

A dark figure in the lower pasture made me choke on the bread. The shadow meandered between the trees.

"Mee-maw!" I yelled through a mouthful of cornbread, which only made me choke and cough more. "Mee-maw, get your gun!"

When I could finally breathe, I raced to her room, feet pounding on the hardwood floors, a drum call to battle. I roused her from her sleep, but she only had to reach out her thin arm and grab the shotgun leanin' against her nightstand.

"What is it?" She shoved her feet into slippers and

marched from her room and out the door. "Is that the lawyer? Leroy? Still pokin' around after all these years?"

She was yammering, and all I could do was point to the lower pasture. The figure was still there, trudging up a small cow trail toward the house.

"That damned man won't ever leave me be!" Her voice shook. "He can't do this to me, not again."

"Mee-maw?"

"Just stay put," she said. "Eat some cornbread."

And I did, nibbling at the buttered edges and pacing until a familiar voice reached my ears. A voice that didn't belong to Mee-maw.

"I want to see her, damn it. I have a right!" the voice bellowed.

"You ain't got no right to be sneakin' and prowling about. Get out of here. I'll shoot you in the leg, mister—and that's *my* right!"

"Lady—"

"Get off my property. Now!" Mee-maw's voice wobbled, and it was hard to determine if it was from frustration or fear.

I waddled with as much authority as a waddling woman could and broke it up. Mee-maw stood on the porch, shotgun poised on her hip, stopping the tall stranger from barreling into the house.

"Mee-maw," I explained, "that's John. He's—"

"—got a right to know what the hell is going on with *that*." John pointed at my belly.

I brushed the crumbs off it. "Hush your mouth, John. You're the baby's daddy." It had to be. The other stories were made of lies and false hope. But hope wasn't enough to change the facts. I sent the letter weeks ago.

"Like hell I am!" he spat, holding up the letter. "What the hell is this, Mae? You send this letter and my wife opens it? She's thinkin' of leaving me with all this. Claiming I have a bastard child. What the hell?"

"You will soon enough." I patted my bump. The kid did a little flip and I imagined it was busy giving John the finger. "Not my fault your wife snoops through your mail, and not my fault she's wisin' up and leaving."

He made a move forward. Mee-maw said nothing but cocked one in the chamber. The *click* of the single barrel Winchester and her hard stare made his feet plant.

He cleared his throat. "What the hell is this about? *Money?* Support for the child? You can't be sure it's mine."

"It is."

"You won't be getting a penny, you tramp. And if you send another letter, I will kill you."

Mee-maw stepped forward, the gun trained on John's chest. "Get out," she said. "Get out. *Now.*"

"Not until this is settled," he said with a sneer.

"I lied earlier," Mee-maw went on. "I wasn't plannin' on shooting you in the leg. I mean, it would've busted it up real good, but this here is full of buckshot. See, I'm not a great aim, so I just figured I'd fill the round with a thousand little pieces of metal and send 'em all flying at once. Some will hit your leg, some'll go through your chest. It really makes a mess. And if you don't wanna be here to witness what picking your own muscle and fat from the dirt is like, I suggest you leave. Tuck that tail and go."

He paused for a few moments before he crumpled the letter and threw it at the porch steps. "Stay out of my life." He turned and marched back down the hill, jumping over the gate and down the gravel road. Mee-maw's eyes never left the back of his head. And when he disappeared into the pasture's treeline, she still didn't move. She only relaxed when the owls started their midnight song—and then, she rounded on me with the same ferocity she had with John. "What the hell were you thinking? I had hope for you! Turns out you just as stupid as your mama."

That stung. I was doing this right, at least planning on it. I was gonna take care of the kid. I wasn't gonna go back to the factories and the men. I was gonna do it right. "You didn't give me a chance to talk with him!"

"You don't need that in your life or the kid's."

"You don't have the right to tell me what I can and cannot do."

She paused. "You're right," she admitted, "but this is my property and I get a right to say who is on it."

I bit my tongue, but not for long and the words fell from my mouth. "And why is it your property, Mee-maw? I *know* the rumors."

She turned and stormed into the house, her slippers stomping and pale pink nightgown glowing in the moonlight. "You're a fool! He only came here because you were asking for money. Your safe place is ruined. He'll come back to finish this whole thing up. How much money were you thinkin', anyway? This a new business plan of yours? How much is a child worth to you?"

I chased after her. "You don't have a right to talk about business plans. Who the hell is Leroy, anyway? Why is he prowling around?"

She turned and grabbed my arm in an icy grip. "Don't you dare utter his name in this house. Now get to bed. Early morning with the cows tomorrow."

"Who is Leroy?"

"None of your concern." She slammed her bedroom door, and I was left in the same place as before, in the kitchen, cornbread in my hand. I stared out the window again, wondering when I'd see John coming for me, and wondering who the hell Leroy was.

I hadn't been sleeping well, and I hated to admit it was because Mee-maw was right. I knew John would come back, and that unsettled me more than the thing kicking inside my belly. My nights at the window grew longer. Shadows of the tree branches were suddenly threats, their long fingers ready to snatch me and my baby away.

"Feeling sick?"

The voice snapped me from my reverie. I spun like a globe and faced Mee-maw, leaning against the kitchen sink. "Ah, I'm fine, just can't sleep is all."

"What are you looking for?" She moved next to me

and slathered butter on a leftover roll. Then she split it and handed the bigger half to me.

"Nothing," I said.

"Don't you lie to me."

I sighed. "What? I just—"

"Want the baby's daddy to come and whisk you away? Come to the rescue? You had to do what your own mama did and find your way out, but she didn't realize the way outta here wasn't lying on your back. Looks like you tried the same, huh?"

The venom in her voice surprised me, but I found myself spitting some of my own. "What do you know of men? What do you know of John or me? And who the hell is Leroy?" The first two questions were involuntary, I didn't want to get into that, not now. I threw that last one in as bait, and she swallowed it whole.

"What do you know of him? He been at you? What did he say?"

"Nothing! Who is he?" I asked, shoving the roll in my mouth hoping it would be enough time for me to think of something else to say. Make her have the hot seat for a moment.

"None of your business." She shoved the roll in her mouth.

We were stuck staring at each other, chewing the bread and butter, a battle of wills. I caved first. "Well, looks like I am gonna have to do my own digging to find out."

Mee-maw went pale. "Don't do that." She put the kettle on, and I knew we were gonna be up until the sun greeted us. We sat across each other on the old oak table

Grandpa built, sipping tea. "Leroy is the son of the only lawyer in town. He wants to make his daddy proud and thinks I came by this property by illegal means. Missing paperwork and such."

"What do you mean?"

"I mean he keeps comin' around, saying I need to sign forms to make this all legal—forms I didn't sign before your grandpa left town. Leroy says this is still in his name and they are gonna seize his property. *My* property."

"Whatever did happen to him? Mee-maw, I know the stories." I asked. I had asked once before, but Mama slapped me silly and hushed me, saying, "He left us—and he's worse than scum. To us, he's dead." So I always figured he was.

"He left," Mee-maw said.

"Seems like a genetic thing." I stared at the weathered kitchen table. There was a deep cut near the edge. I'd made it when I was just a little thing, maybe six or seven. I don't know why I did it.

"Ah, yes. The women in our line pick the bad ones, don't we?" Mee-maw sipped her tea.

"What made you choose Grandpa?" I asked. I'd never met him, and it felt strange to call him that.

"Your mama," Mee-maw said. "Pregnant at sixteen . . . What else was I supposed to do?"

Run away, I thought. "I dunno," I said.

Mee-maw huffed. "I'm sorry about the boy's father."

The comment made my heart fall and soar at once. "You think it's a boy?"

"Look at the way you're carryin'. Of course, it's a boy."

I rubbed my belly. "Don't be sad about his daddy. No good, anyhow." And I found myself meaning it. My resolve holding firmer. I could tell him his daddy was killed in a work accident. Maybe he got sick and died. I could be the next Mee-maw. Strong and independent, I could have men in my life the way I chose. I'd be around for the baby that way.

Mee-maw set her tea down. "Your grandpa was a vile man. The only thing he did right was teaching me how to aim a gun proper, to keep the varmints away from the chickens." She stood and set her plate in the sink. She pulled on her muck boots and jacket. "I'm gonna get a head start on the day." She left the warm house and walked into the darkness, to the comfort of her cows.

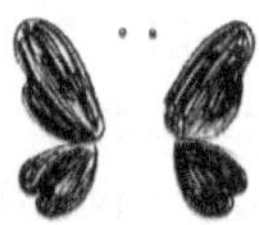

I still wasn't sleeping well. The baby was kicking hard, and the growing discomfort of it was my constant companion. I stood by the kitchen window, bread in one hand, tea in the other. I stared out at the moonlit pasture, at the giant tree. I replayed the last few weeks, regretting the final letter I sent to John. It was a moment of weakness. I so badly wanted some nice things for the baby, and the little I'd saved would not cover it. I just wanted a little something—he owed me that much. None of his time, energy, nothin'. Just a spot of cash for a crib and new blankets.

I regretted it as soon as I sent it.

I jumped at every creak and groan of the house. The whisper of the wind caused my skin to prickle. A figure in the pasture made me freeze, but it only took a moment to realize it was Mee-maw, her long nightgown swaying in the summer breeze. Her thin arms carried a stick—no, a shovel. She wandered that base of the tree, meandering between the shadows created by the moon. Then, footsteps creaked across the old kitchen floor and my blood ran cold. They were heavy, like a man wearing boots.

"Thought I told you to get out of my business." It was John's voice, but it was low, seething, and crackling like fire.

I spun, grabbing what I could in my hand, but he slapped the butterknife away as soon as his eyes locked with mine. He wore old jeans and a t-shirt. Gloves on his hands. The sound of the butterknife clattering to the floor rang in my ears.

"Mee—" My shout was cut off by his hands to my throat.

"I told you not to send me no more letters."

He squeezed. I clawed at his hand, his arm, *anything*, scratching his skin away.

"Two less things to worry about," he said, using both hands to squeeze. My arms went limp, my head spun, and black spots swirled. The ringing in my ears reached a fever pitch. My world was going dark and the last thing I would look at was his scrunched-up, red face.

And then, it was over. I could breathe. I was warm, the blood coming back to my body—and I was sticky. Warm, red goo covered my arms and face.

Mee-maw stood, gun poised on her hip, her frail arms shaking, her light pink gown spattered with red. John lay crumpled at my feet, his head a mass of oozing meat.

"Told you I knew how to shoot varmints."

"No buckshot in that one?" I asked. My voice was hoarse, raw, burning.

"Never use buckshot on critters," she said. Her voice was monotone; she stared at the heap of a man on the floor.

And reality hit. Tears welled in my eyes.

"You all right?" Mee-maw asked, resting the gun against the wall.

I nodded, rubbing my throat. "He was gonna kill me."

"He sure was gonna try. Good thing you're so full of hot air—I knew you'd be able to hang on long enough." She shuffled over, her slippers soaking up the quickly spreading blood. She touched my arm. "I'm glad you're okay." I'd never seen Mee-maw cry. I didn't that night either, but it was as close as she'd gotten.

"What do we do with him?" I asked.

Mee-maw pointed out the kitchen window, to the lone tree in the pasture. "Bury him with the rest."

BIRTHDAY BALLOONS

He had seventy-seven balloons to blow up—all for his own birthday party. One might consider inflating balloons a punishment. But the ladies banished him and his two eldest granddaughters to the living room, instructed not to leave until exactly seventy-seven were inflated, he considered it a win. It was certainly better than hanging streamers.

"It's for the balloon wall," his eldest granddaughter said.

"Whatever you say, Silly Sarah," he said. "What do you think about it all, Loony Lucy?"

The second eldest huffed, staring at the box. "Looks like a lot. Better get cracking."

"Dibs on the pink one!" he said, reaching into the box between them. "Pink for my first daughter."

"Should I do blue for my dad?" Loony Lucy asked.

"Only if Sarah does red for the first rose bush I

planted out front." He threw a thumb over his shoulder and Sarah grabbed the red balloon.

"What next?" Lucy asked, catching her breath and tying off the balloon.

"Both of you should grab a pink next, one for each of you." He picked up a green one. "I'll do this for your brother—he's the only smart one, out hiding in the garden or something."

They raced each other; Sarah won this time.

"What next?" Sarah asked, breathing just as hard as Lucy had been.

"One green and one white." He picked up a balloon from the box. "And gold for me! The colors of Colorado State University. And now I've got a head start."

The girls scrabbled for the colors and nearly beat him, but he tied his off just in time. And so the game went. Lucy had purple balloon for the heart he received in the war. Sarah did four orange ones in a row, one for each sunset he saw at the beach. Colorado didn't have many beaches afterall. He grabbed two yellows, one for each Labrador he had growing up. He picked a gold one next, for the golden retriever begging the ladies for scraps right now.

"What next?"

"Grab a blue one," he said, "for that time your grandma dyed her hair and it didn't look too right."

The girls giggled and Lucy picked up a purple one. "Here's one for when she tried to fix it!"

He laughed at that one and picked up a green next. "For when I visited the tallest tree in the states." Then he exchanged it for a red one—the tree had been a redwood, after all.

And they played the game some more. Sarah grabbed a white one for his degree in biology. Lucy chose a blue one for his favorite fishing spot. He took a purple one for his favorite merlot.

The scattered balloons began to fill the space between the couches, flooding into the hallway. Seventy-seven was quite a lot.

"Last one," Sarah said.

"Glad you were counting," he said.

"You do the honors," Lucy said, batting the inflated balloons out of the way of the box. "Oh, how lucky—just one left, too!" She reached a hand in and held up the last balloon.

"That's not a very nice color," Sarah muttered.

"And the only one in the whole box," Lucy said.

"A black one," he said. "I guess that's part of life too." He took it from Lucy's hand.

"Don't," Lucy said. "It's not a good one."

"What is this one for?" Sarah asked.

For me? Thought the grandfather. For the sins sitting on my shoulder?

"We all have a little gray in our lives," he explained. The girls didn't respond.

He blew it up, and with the last breath made the girls jump when it popped. He paused for a moment and laughed; the girls giggled with him, their laughter music to his soul, and he thought his heart might burst. He glanced at the fragments of latex on the floor and thought it probably would.

WHAT'S IN A NAME?

I hated first dates. And I have had more of those than any other kind. Nothing more I could do but go on a few more.

Johnathon. As I searched through my wardrobe, I rolled his name over my tongue. "Johnathon." What does that name warrant in the world of fashion? Something preppy. *Johnathon would have gone to a prep school, I'm sure. Should I match him? Maybe try an outfit some of the schoolgirls wore? Maybe I can bring him back to his youth.*

I wrinkled my nose at my collared blouses and little skirts. Not my style. But it did seem fitting for a Johnathon...

My phone chimed, a message from him. It was sent through the dating app we connected on. "Excited to see you! I will be running a few minutes late, though. Sorry!" It was followed by a laughing face emoji. A smile spread across my face.

I wasn't upset about him running late. If anything, it showed his boyishness. He was probably getting back and hurrying to change from an unexpected soccer match or something. The emoji helped too. He probably went by Johnny. I tried it out. "Johnny." Oh, that was something playful.

I threw the old options on the ground and reached for a colorful print. Something strappy and young. I vacillated between a few options before I settled on the blue floral print sundress. Light and fun; something fitting for a "Johnny."

When I arrived at the restaurant, I went to our table and sat, smoothing out my pretty dress, waiting for Johnny to show. And then the thought struck me. *What if he is a "John?" What if he is a plain old businessman?*

I suddenly felt too young, too flirty. My flowy dress was just so out of place for a "John." I wrapped my jacket over my bare shoulders.

"Hey, are you Lindsay?" a voice asked.

"Yeah!" I beamed, standing. He took his seat. I sat back down.

"Sorry I'm late—you know how it goes."

I nodded and tried not to laugh uncomfortably. "Yeah," I said. "Gave me time to look at the menu and what not."

"I heard this place is good." He looked around. He must've been close to my age—no facial hair and only a slight receding hairline. I shed my coat. Then, we ordered. It was a nice way to talk, just not to each other.

"Your Instagram made you seem fun, so when you

suggested his place, I thought I'd give it a try." He wrinkled his nose. "To each their own, I guess."

I laughed and took a drink of my wine to fill the space. *He seems more like a Johnathon. Maybe I should have worn the polo.* I dug a little further. "So, what do you do for fun? I used to play loads of tennis when I was in college, even had a fair bit of time playing golf."

He smiled wide. *Maybe he is a Johnny after all.* "I love soccer. Played all through school, even college." He scanned me up and down. "You look like you were in great shape when you were younger." He took a big swig of wine. "You could start playing again—maybe look more like your old pics."

"Thanks," I said, taking another drink. I fought the urge to pull my coat back on.

Not a John, but unclear as to Johnathon or Johnny. I gave up on guessing and finally asked. "So, do you prefer Johnathon, John, or Johnny?"

"Actually, Johnathon is my dad's name. I go by my middle name: Richard."

Of course. He's a Dick.

A FAMILY KNIFE

"Here, honey," Granny said. "I think it's time you have this."

The girl took the small package in her hands. She unwrapped the string and tore away the paper. "A knife?"

"Not just any knife," Granny said with a smile. "This used to be my own mama's. Every girl must have their own paring knife when they get older. Happy birthday. This one is yours now."

"What does it do?" The girl flipped it in her hand; the wooden handle was smooth and shiny from years of use.

"It's a sharp knife. Every good girl needs one. It's to cut your sentences short, to make it easier for people to understand you. It's to clip your dreams just a touch smaller, to make them more reasonable. Attainable, you see?"

The girl didn't, but she nodded anyway. Was the knife already doing its job?

Granny went on. "You'll want to slice little bits of your heart away too—the broken and bruised bits." The girl nodded silently. Granny looked down at her, smiling. "Slice and dice that anger and frustration you have so they are in nice bite-sized pieces. It's easier to hide that way."

The girl swallowed hard. "And sadness?"

"You can cut those into nice thin strips. People aren't so frightened by that. Just not too much, though. You'll also want to cut away the pieces of you that are too big."

"What is the right size?" The girl asked, clutching the knife.

"Oh, just less." Granny smiled wide.

"It sounds like this will just cut my life short."

"Oh, it will." Granny ran a finger over the smooth handle. "But that's just the right size."

And Granny wandered off, talking about chopping and dicing.

"Happy birthday, girlie," Auntie said.

The girl pocketed the small knife and opened the long package her aunt placed in front of her. "A machete?"

"To cut down anyone who stands in your way and to cut kindling to stoke your own fire," Auntie said.

The machete was far heavier than the little knife. But it felt so much better in her hand, but it didn't feel *right*.

So the girl handed the heavy knife back. "I think you better keep this. You still have fires to stoke."

"But you still need something," Auntie said.

The girl nodded and slipped between family and friends, busy chatting and eating cake. She knelt by Granny's crochet basket and dug around, looking for a box. She opened the frayed cardboard container and pulled out a shiny, sharp needle no bigger than her thumb.

"What will you use that for?" Auntie asked, clutching the machete at her side.

"It's to stitch back together hearts. To piece together dreams. To thread together big words and sentences."

"It's not very big."

"It's to poke holes in arguments, to fix broken pieces. To stitch wounds. Sew new things." It was a small and dainty thing, but it felt perfect in her hand.

CARD GAME

They sat across from each other at the barren kitchen table. Years of scratches and dents in the oak were enough decoration. It fit perfectly among the floral wallpaper and dusty china cabinet.

"Grandma, it's your turn," the kid said, nudging the stack of cards in front of him. The sticky deck was the only bridge between the generations.

"Right." The old woman smiled. "What do they call you again?"

The kid looked at his mother. She gave him a small smile and nod from where she sat on the couch, making it clear she was a spectator in this strange sport.

"Roman," he said. The pangs of sadness over her forgetting his name shifted to pricks of annoyance over these last months. He used to explain his relation, voice shaking from fear and frustration. How could someone forget him?

Now he didn't care.

Her wrinkled hands took a card from the top and the old woman tucked it in next to the few in her hand. When Roman went to reach for a card, she said, "Oh no, mister." She tutted and spread her cards across the table.

Roman stared, counting off the cards once, twice. "You cheated!" he said, standing so fast the chair scraped across the floor. He dashed to the other side of the table where he pointed and exclaimed, "See! You hid the cards on your lap! On your apron!"

"Oh." The white-haired woman gave a toothy grin and her eyes almost disappeared in the wrinkles. "How'd you know?"

Roman shrugged. "'Cause those aren't the ones I gave you."

VANILLA SMOKE

Granddaddy always talked about dying. He yelled, "I don't wanna die here!" or "I'm going home to die like I want."

"You're already home, Grandaddy," Jackson said. "Just die here."

"It won't be the same 'sperience," Grandaddy said.

Jackson shrugged and so did his Mama. She whispered to Jackson, "Don't pay him no mind. His own mind's been lost awhile."

But Grandaddy took to carrying an old valise around with him. He kept it by his door each night and carried it to the kitchen when he woke for his morning coffee. By the time Mama caught him trying to sneak out, he'd made it down the street, that old valise clutched tight in his wrinkled hand.

"What you got in there, Daddy?" Mama asked him when she managed to herd him back inside.

"All the things I need." He opened it, pulling out a jar

of tobacco and his spare pipe with unsteady hands. He had a small, half-used bottle of Cornhuskers liniment. The clear liquid had probably been in there for decades; Granddaddy hadn't needed to use it for his dry, cracked hands in a while.

"Where you trying to go?" Jackson asked.

The whole suitcase smelled of tobacco. Grandaddy took the jar and popped it open, stuffing a small bundle in the pipe he kept in his pocket. He didn't light it, just inhaled the scent. "Smell that, Jacky boy?"

"Smells like tobacco."

"And?"

Jackson took another sniff. "Sweetness?"

"That's the vanilla. And that's where I'm going. Back home. Back where my blood and sweat seeped into soil and became part of the earth. Seems only right that I die there too."

Mama came in from the kitchen, holding a tray of lemonade. "That tobacco farm is long gone, Daddy. Sold to another farmer. I think it's an orchard of some kind now. Fruit trees. Much better for you, anyway."

"I know, I know." Granddaddy grew agitated, squirming in his seat, like he was fixing to run some-where. Like he was in church. "But it's there. That place of my boyhood, my early manhood. I met your Grammy there. She birthed you, honey, right in the grass out back since you just couldn't wait to make an entrance to this world. You're part of the land, too—blood and tears and all."

Mama let out a heavy sigh. "That house is gone now. That farming part of you is gone, too. Why did you work so hard to get out of the farming life, to make something more for all of us, if you just wanna go back there?"

Grandaddy didn't say anything. He carefully packed the jar back in the valise and shuffled away to his room, bent and crooked, like the branches of an old oak tree. "It's not far to go," Grandaddy mumbled. "Not far at all."

Jackson sipped his lemonade, inhaling the lingering scent of that vanilla tobacco in the air.

Mama looked like she bit into a lemon. "He gets like this when the sun starts to set. Unsettled like. I don't know why he'd want to go back. We left that place and never returned, never crossed my mind to. Same with your grammy. She chose to die out here, away from that part of her life. They got me an education, got me a life outside the fields."

Jackson nodded, finding it rather strange that people got to choose where they died. He thought the river would be a good place for him—but then again, if he died at this house, he could still walk around it as a ghost. Mama took in a deep breath, and it looked like the vanilla tobacco settled her nerves.

But when Jackson woke up, there was a noticeable freshness about the place. The lingering scent of smoke cleared away. And Mama was scared. Jackson was too.

"Where's Granddaddy?"

"I don't know." Mama was already ambling outside, searching the streets, hoping to catch him on his way outta town again.

Jackson took a peek in Granddaddy's room. The old valise was gone, and Jackson knew Grandaddy was too.

When Mama came back, sweating and fretting, she

grabbed her keys, shoving Jackson in the backseat with just his pajamas and socks on. "Come help me look."

They circled the neighborhood, then their side of town, then the entire town. Mama tried her best to drive through the tears.

"Let's go to his dying place," Jackson suggested.

"It's way too far away," Mama said.

"But he isn't here," Jackson said. "Maybe he caught a bus or left a long time ago."

Mama swallowed hard and turned the car around. And hours went by. The roads turned to gravel and eventually a long line of trees came into view.

"This is it," Mama whispered. "I swore I'd never be back here." She slowed the car to a crawl, and they limped along that pothole-filled road. "Not fruit trees," Mama muttered. "They're chestnut trees."

She pulled the car to the side of the road and stepped out. Jackson followed close behind.

"Daddy!" Mama yelled. A flock of birds scattered but there was no other answer. "Up there, at that crossroad, is where the shack used to be," Mama said.

Jackson nodded and followed in Mama's footsteps, searching the rows of endless trees for Granddaddy, dodging potholes in his slippers.

"It used to sit right here," Mama explained. "There were a few other shacks along this road here, too. They were all the same, but ours had a covered porch, thanks to Daddy's handiwork. Lord, I swore I'd never come back. Grammy, too. They said they didn't want to see my spine mangled and hands ruined. That's why I went to school, and you will too. Be whatever you want." Mama rambled when she was nervous. "You could be a doctor, a teacher, heck, even a businessman and do whatever they do, you'd do it best. I know you would. Why would he come back? Why?"

"Mama, look." Jackson picked up a pipe from the side of the road, still warm with orange embers glowing inside.

"Daddy?" Mama called out again.

And he replied in the form of a breeze that smelled just like vanilla smoke.

MILK DELIVERY

Most people fail to realize that housewives in the fifties couldn't just pop onto a computer and order their heart's desires. They didn't have a magical machine take their money and spit out their goods on the front porch. They didn't have a machine to wash their clothes or dishes. No, they used to brave the markets and the malls and the Sears frenzies, but that wasn't all—they also used the door-to-door salesmen. And Lottie used them all.

Lottie Spring was soon known as the house to start your route with. Or end at. Or just be at. She'd invite them in and let them perform their sales pitch. She'd smile and nod and laugh and smile, and they'd leave zipping up their pants, eager to come back next week, even if she didn't buy anything.

You see, she balanced the checkbook. She purchased the things for the house, the things she needed—and, well, her husband wouldn't sleep with her. Said he cared *too much* about her, that *respected* her so much. Instead, he slept with his nurses. The barmaids. Hotel staff when he traveled—which was nearly every weekend. Strange how those medical conferences always landed on a Saturday. But Lottie managed the house and herself just fine.

Lottie subscribed to *Colliers*. The young man who took her order showed up right on time each week to deliver the magazines. He was inexperienced. This was his first job and all. He was inexperienced in other ways, but his enthusiasm was all Lottie needed to make up for the fact. But when it was time to renew her subscription, she realized there wasn't much she hadn't already read, experienced, and seen. Her subscription lapsed, but the boy occasionally stopped by for a delivery anyway.

The Milkman was always prompt for his deliveries. And she didn't mind entertaining him, either. He was full of surprises and made his weekly delivery well worth the wait.

The ladies in the neighborhood knew. Of course, they knew. Lottie didn't care. Mrs. Wilson wanted to tattle, but what proof did she have? She let her suspicions take root in the mouths of the other ladies on the block. The neighborhood entertainment was sitting on the porch, drinking sweet tea, and watching Lottie Spring's revolving front door.

Mrs. Loretta loved the scandal and often waited by the window to see just how long Lottie entertained the milkman. Five minutes seemed awfully fast. Or was it slow? She couldn't really tell. Though on other weeks, it was nearly an hour.

Susie—the young woman across the street—lived alone. Her husband was deployed, over in Korea, doing whatever soldiers do. Susie came over when the Milkman left, sobbing. (She was privy to the schedule, just like Mrs. Loretta.)

"He has a girl—a concubine!" the young wife wailed.

Doing whatever soldiers do, Lottie thought. But Lottie smiled knowingly and slid the stack of *Collier* magazines across the table. Lottie renewed the subscription, a gift for her young friend. Susie seemed much happier after her weekly delivery. The young man was made of testosterone and inexperience, so it was an easy change to his route, to give him something new to try.

But three months later, Susie came back to Lottie's house, fresh tears wetting her face. "I'm pregnant!" she cried.

Lottie inwardly laughed at the young soldier's punishment. She almost found herself wishing she could give her own husband a similar sort of beating. Almost. Her next feeling was more empathetic. She helped young Susie pen a letter, the perfect mix of heartache and disappointment at her husband's sin, and regret for how she handled the news. Pure poetry—it was the perfect "I'm sorry you made this happen" letter.

Three months after that, Lottie got to watch from her porch swing (she wasn't the only entertainment of the neighborhood, after all) as a young soldier stepped out of a cab, duffle bag over his shoulder. He stiffened when he saw his wife, already stepping onto the sidewalk.

Then he strode toward her, putting his hands on her belly. Lottie smiled.

She left the pair and went back inside to pull out the pie. It had just enough time to cool before the brand-new Milkman made his delivery.

INVEST-MINTS

Mama made Gramps come and live with us. He lived in the city and when he fell too many times, and Mama had him delivered to us like a package—he even came wrapped in a wrinkled brown coat, looking just like frail, crumpled wrapping paper. He had a lot of stuff, but apparently he had way more back in 'cago.

"Donnie boy, I moved to 'cago when I was twenty-two. Had a dollar to my name and now look where I am. Back where I started. They took my house."

"Your house is still there, Dad. It's being rented out to a nice tenant. It's still yours."

"You kidnapped me and brought me here. You're keeping me hostage. Way out in the middle of nowhere. These murky bogs are gonna swallow me whole."

"There are no bogs here, Dad!" Mama yelled from inside the kitchen.

"Then where the hell do all these flies come from?"

"I don't know!" Mama hollered. "Wherever they come from!"

Mama yelled at me the same way she did her own Daddy, and I liked that Gramps and I were on an even playing field.

Gramps pointed at me. "Donnie, in the cities there are rats and rascals all over the streets, but none of these damn flies in my lemonade."

"That's not lemonade," I said.

"Don't tell your mother," Gramps hissed. "A thousand flies are buzzing around me." He tried to flick them away, but his hands were too slow.

"There's not that many. It just happens in the summer."

"It's 'cause of all those damn cows and their shit lying around, festering. Stinking up the wind. How do you stink up the wind? Live on a farm."

"But you like steak," I said. Gramps was just annoyed. He was with everything.

"Not when I have to fight off flies for a flank." Every time he used a word starting with "f," spittle flew from his lips. "Tell you what, Donnie boy, I have a proposition for you."

"Mama said I ain't allowed to have any of those."

"Oh, shut it. A proposition. A job. I will pay you one cent for each fly you kill and bring to me. No cheating, now. I'm gonna count every single one of 'em."

Donnie scampered off; it seemed like the best time to escape. And what was he gonna do all day, anyway? He swiped a jar of peaches from the pantry—the ones way far back, so Mama wouldn't notice. He ate them with his fingers in the barn, letting the cows lick the sugar from his hands when he was through. When the jar was finally empty, he set to work, scouring the cobwebs in the barn, picking the flies from the webs. Some might have been globs of dirt, but they could pass at flies. He went inside after that, filling the jar with bugs from the windowsill.

He pulled the legs off a dried spider and thought it would fool Gramps. And then the fun began. He grabbed the old kitchen towel—Mama called it a tea towel, but they never had any of that dirty water in the house, so he didn't think she'd miss it. Donnie made his way to the watering trough; there were always flies buzzing around the cow water.

It took him a few tries, but eventually he figured it out. It was all in the wrist, snapping the tea towel at the flies. But he got tired and took to swatting lazily at the flies. Every time he knocked one to the dirt, he carefully pinched it and dropped it in his jar, careful to keep it as fly-like as possible. He didn't think Gramps would *actually* count them, but better safe than sorry.

"What on earth are you doing, Donald?" a shrill voice asked.

He'd been so preoccupied with the fly swatting he'd missed the signature thumping footsteps of his older cousin.

"What you want with me, Lois?"

"For you to tell me what you're doing. You being punished for something? Did you forget to close the pasture gate again?"

"What?" Donnie stood and faced her. "Why would you think that?"

"Well, last time you got a wild hair and spit at your sister, your mama made you spit until the mason jar was full. You were crying like a baby, telling everyone you were gonna die of thirst. At least Aunt June didn't make you drink it."

"I'm not in trouble." Donnie turned back to the water trough. The flies were gone. Lois's high-pitched voice was probably scaring them away.

"Gramps said he'd pay me a whole cent for each fly I caught."

"That is so stupid!" She laughed and hollered and sat on her butt, picking the grass from between her toes. She never wore shoes in the summer. But Donnie could tell she was interested. "Everyone knows a fly ain't worth a penny."

"I know," Donnie said. "But may as well see if he'll stick to it. He hates liars, you know, and if I even come close to calling him one, I'm sure he'll pay up."

"I'm gonna help you."

"No, you're not," Donnie said, slapping at a rogue grasshopper. He contemplated taking off the legs and pretending it was a fly, but it wasn't the right color. Even Gramps's bad eyes would know it was a fake.

"Of course, I am." Lois stood, pushing the rogue curls from her face. She cocked a hip. She was only two years older than Donnie, but she towered over him.

"Fine," Donnie said. "Just know you're only getting paid for what you bring in and I won't lose count."

"So . . ." She crouched low, taking the new role of fly snatcher seriously. "Is this your mama's daddy?"

"It's my Gramps."

"No," she hissed, as if that would help the flies. "I mean, we have Grandpa Allen—that's your daddy's and my daddy's dad. So, this one must be your mom's."

"Well, of course," Donnie said. In truth, that whole explanation really cleared up a lot of questions for Donnie. He didn't know why they had to share one grandpa but not the other.

They spent most of the day chasing flies and found a great deal by the old scraps at the chicken coop. They even found some dead ones stuck in cobwebs by the woodpile.

"Let's go see what your gramps has to say!" Lois said.

They had half a mason jar full of the dead, little things. They almost looked like raisins, and Donnie's stomach turned at the thought of fresh baked oatmeal raisin cookies. He'd never be able to eat them again.

"What are you two making a fuss about?" Gramps asked from his same spot on the porch. "Who are you?" He pointed to Lois.

"That's my cousin," Donnie said. "I told you about her."

"Ah," Gramps said, nodding. "The one that talks too much and sneezes like a banshee. She's the one that fell asleep in church and farted so loud it made the preacher stop preachin', right?"

Donnie's face flamed and he knew Lois would push him in the river for that. Or in front of a train. Her pink cheeks turned crimson.

"No," Lois said sweetly, "that would be the girl Donnie fancies. *Linda.*"

"Right." Gramps gave Donnie a wink. "What you got in that jar?"

"Flies!" Donnie said proudly, holding it up for him.

"Huh," was all Gramps said. He took the tray from the side table that had the remains of his dinner on it and tossed the plates aside. He dumped the contents of the jar across the table and took out a pen, separating the dried little flies into neat piles. "This one don't count." He tossed it aside. "Any fool can see it's been dead for weeks. I wanted fresh ones." He tossed another speck aside. "That's a spider." He continued sorting, muttering, "Can't believe you went and did it."

When he was done with his sorting, he counted the piles by twenty-five. Donnie didn't even know that was possible. The biggest he was taught in school so far was by tens. Counting by twos was the hardest.

"Two hundred and four. And if I am being honest, I think four of those might be spiders or some other insect, so—" Gramps pulled out his billfold and unwrinkled some bills. He handed two to Donnie. "Two whole dollars."

"Thank you!" Donnie said. "Can I do it again?"

"Sure," Grandpappy grunted. "But you won't get as many now that they're all gone from the windowsill."

Donnie looked sheepish for a moment.

"That's right, I know about that—problem is, I can't tell which ones are old. Just know I'm watching. Our deal still stands. A penny for a fly."

Donnie scooped up the jar and ran out to the water

trough, hoping dusk might draw out more flies. Lois was on his heels and they both ignored the complaints of Gramps wondering what he was gonna do with a whole tray of dead flies.

"All right, give me the dollars," Lois said.

"No way!" Donnie said, stuffing them in his back pocket. "You only caught thirty-two. That's—" He did the math in his head. Good thing he could count by tens and twos. "Thirty-two cents."

"I know, I know," Lois said, huffing. She stood like she always did when she was about to make a speech. Feet together, hands folded in front. A serious pout on her face. "I want to explain something to you. Something grown-ups talk about—"

"Oh, *gross*—"

"It's not that!" Lois stood, her hand on her hip now. "It's this thing called invest-mints. It's this thing you do. You give your money to someone and then they give it back with even more money. They make your money, make more money, and then you both get to keep the extra."

"We learned about that in Sunday school," Donnie said, stuffing the dollars deeper in his pocket. "This isn't like the miracles with the oil and water and stuff. And the fish and bread."

"No," Lois crossed her arms. "This is real. I hear people do it all the time. And I think I can do it. In fact —" She gave Donnie a nice smile. "In fact, I am *so* sure that if I take your money now, this time next week if I don't give you your two dollars and more back, I'll clean out the chicken coop for you any time your mama asks you to do it . . . for the next *year*."

She was dumber than Gramps, at least that was what Donnie was thinking. He had those crinkled bills out of his pocket and into her hand so fast he barely had time to consider if getting more dollars would be worth it. He almost wanted her to be stuck with the awful chore of cleaning out the coop.

"Why are they called invest-mints?" Donnie asked. It was a logical question after all. And he thought he ought to put up more of a fight, some sort of resistance and all of that, keep *some* pride.

"Cause people go and buy mints with them at the drugstore. 'Dults love mints. We can buy other stuff, though, they're not just for mints." She smoothed out the bills in her hands.

It seemed to make sense, and Donnie nodded. If he had to buy mints, he supposed chewing gum would count.

"Say, would you be willing to extend the days, just a bit? Today's Saturday and all. Could we do it Sunday, after church? Not tomorrow's Sunday, but the next Sunday? So really it would be eight days, kind of. I suppose it would be seven days plus a few hours. Wait, hang on—"

"That's fine. Sunday after church you can give me the two dollars and more." Donnie said. She could tell she was edging into the area where math was involved, and he wanted to get out of that warzone sooner than later. "I just hope you don't mind the smell of chicken poo and rotten veggies. Just so you know, Mama asks me to clean it once every few weeks." He smiled at the thought of Lois covered in chicken gunk.

They went their separate ways. He saw Lois at church the next day, but they weren't in the Sunday school class together anymore. She was big and sat with the 'dults. She didn't look too worried about the invest-mints, but he supposed that was a good sign. Either he'd be richer for doing nothing or he'd be happier for not doing the coop cleanings. It was a win-win.

He fought the urge to collect flies all week. He wanted to see what Lois would do. Plus it was near the end of hay season, so he was in the field picking up the broken bales for most of the day anyway and there weren't many flies out there.

Mama was surprised when Donnie was up and ready for church the following week. Normally she had to drag him out by his ear, usually wiping his face in the truck with the hem of her dress as they tumbled inside the small building. But today he was at the breakfast table, eating with Gramps, swatting the flies away from his eggs. Donnie slapped one flat. "That's a penny for me, Gramps."

The old man grunted, shooing another fly away. "I only take 'em in increments of a hundred. Ninety-nine more to go."

Donnie shrugged. That didn't seem like too much of a challenge with how busy the little bugs were this morning. But he wanted to see what Lois had up her sleeve, how she could make magic and turn two dollars into more. Still, he put the smashed fly in his pocket anyway.

He had to wait all through Sunday school. He tried to get Lois's attention when he walked to Sunday school, but she ignored him. Donnie was kind of disappointed the magic didn't work, until he realized he would be off coop duty for a while.

But after service, when there was that long, painful amount of time where the 'dults stood around talking in the foyer with coffee or out in the parking lot, Lois found him.

"Come with me," she said. There was a big smile on her face.

Donnie glanced at her pockets, but it didn't look like she had stacks of coins or bills stuffed in them. "Did you do it?" Donnie asked. "Make the invest-mints?"

"Come and see."

He knew by her triumphant grin that she had done it. "Where's the money? How much is it? Are we gonna go buy some mints now or something?"

She grabbed his hand and they raced through the dirt parking lot. He had been so preoccupied that he hadn't realized that most of the kids he played tag with after service were nowhere to be seen. And then he saw them. A line of kids holding their mason jars and carefully placing them in the back of his Pa's truck. Jimmy and Jenny hauled over an entire milk crate full of jars.

After each kid put their loot in the bed of the truck, Lois handed out pennies and nickels like candy. She elbowed Donnie in the side, "ten cents for every hundred." She winked. "Can you believe it?"

Donnie was shocked. "But we get paid more."

"Hush, Donald," Lois chided. "Everyone knows a hundred flies ain't worth that much, it's a steal for them."

Donnie had to agree. If he was given the same offer, he'd be out catching flies for ten cents on the hundred.

"How are you counting them all?" Donnie asked.

"Just gotta trust them," Lois said in a real serious voice, handing Reggie a twenty-five-cent piece. "Plus, I told 'em all they'd burn in hell for lying since we are at church."

Fair enough. "But these aren't bills. You're giving away the money."

"Oh, you're thick!" Lois said.

Not really, Donnie thought. If anything, he'd been aiming to pack some more meat on his bones.

"You'll see when we take 'em back to your place."

"Whatever you say," Donnie said, running a finger over his ribs. Nope, not thick at all. "But Mama usually asks me to clean the coop on Tuesdays."

Mama asked about the jars on the way home. "They're a joke with Gramps," Donnie said. Mama looked like she wanted to know more but then thought better of it. Lois hitched a ride with them back and she and Mama talked about how *awful* it was that Eunice couldn't run the potluck next week.

When they pulled into the drive, Pa parked a little ways off the front path, not in his usual spot in the barn. He gave Donnie and Lois a wink. "To help you unload faster."

"Thanks, Uncle Ben. See, Donnie? He knows what we're up to. Now help me unload. Where's your gramps anyway?"

"I think Mama went to make him lunch. He usually eats it on the porch since he says it's too stuffy inside." Which Donnie had to admit was strange; there was hardly anyone ever inside.

Donnie helped unload the jars. There were lots of them. Maybe twelve jars and a few cans, mostly full of flies.

"I told them about this last Sunday," Lois explained. "I didn't think they'd go this crazy, but I'm not complaining. Never underestimate the power of farm kids, free time, and candy cash on the line."

"I still don't—"

"Oh, look! Here he comes," Lois said.

Right on cue, Gramps shuffled out the front door, letting the screen slam behind him—which wasn't very fair to Donnie, though, because he always got yelled at when he slammed it.

"What in tarnation are you doing?" Gramps asked as he sat on his favorite place on the porch. He pulled the tray that was sitting on the little side table onto his lap and dug into his sandwich while he stared at the pair.

"Got you some more flies," Donnie said, realization finally clicking. *We're rich!*

Gramps grunted. "How many?"

Donnie looked to Lois, who whispered, "At least a thousand."

"About a thousand," Donnie said with a smile. "Maybe two."

Grandpappy stopped chewing. In fact, he was still for so long that Donnie was afraid he up and died, got instant mortis, and was stiff and cold. Finally, he cleared his throat. "I guess I better get to counting."

And in the end, Donnie and Lois ended up with six dollars and twelve cents. *Each.* But Grandpappy said the deal was off after that. And just for the hell of it, Donnie bought some mint chewing gum.

SALT

Rufus was never good at school. He was never liked by his teachers. And that's why he was always picked first. The teachers liked to watch him squirm, they let him be the example of what not to do so the other kids wouldn't feel embarrassed. He stood up when the teacher called on him and he thought about the question real hard. He'd have a great answer and maybe he'd move down on the shit list a line or two. Maybe become one of the invisible students or something.

But it was a big question. Fourth grade was when they started asking the real hard stuff. There was a lot to choose from, and Rufus was sure his classmates didn't know half as many as he did.

He could go with a classic, like garlic powder, or maybe something more obscure, like smoked paprika. Or he could change his voice and giggle out "spicy," and make his classmates laugh, or speak with a lisp and say "cinnamon" or "sassafras."

Still, he bit his lip as the eyes of the teacher rested on him. It sounded basic, but salt was his favorite. Salt flavored everything; salt held it all together. At least that was what Grandma said. Salt preserved things. Salt *saved* things. Salt put out fires, it soothed bee stings—at least Grandma claimed that too.

Salt was a little bit of magic; it perfected anything fried, and it fixed anything Mom tried to cook. One time Grandma was crying over the pot, big crocodile tears falling into the chili. "Don't mind the extra salt, dear," Grandma had said. "Just adds extra flavor."

And that chili was *good*, the best Rufus had ever eaten. Everyone was putting extra tears in their chili, Rufus too. It used to be Grandad's favorite. They didn't eat chili anymore.

"Rufus?" his teacher asked, tapping the desk. "Your answer?"

"Salt," Rufus said.

Some kids groaned, some snickered, some rolled their eyes, but there was a chorus of giggles and chuckles.

Teacher rubbed her head. "Favorite *season*, Rufus."

MUSTACHE

My Uncle Gus had wiry gray hair. I was told used to be black. He also had a mustache, a giant monstrosity sitting on his upper lip. At least that's what Aunt Linda called it. Apparently, the hairy thing used to be black too, but now it was white with tinges of yellow from the tobacco. Uncle Gus always messed with the mustache, testing it constantly, checking to make sure the long ends were waxed into a perfect curl. Aunt Linda *hated* it. She always told us that if Uncle Gus touched her like he touched his damn mustache, they might have actually had a kid or two. She always said this when there were lots of people around and it always made everyone as uncomfortable as Uncle Gus's mustache fondling.

Uncle Gus and Aunt Linda always came over for the Easter stuff. They stayed in one of the many guest rooms. It was tradition to cram as many people into the house as possible and get exhausted by the time everyone left. Mom would swear she'd never host Easter weekend again and then she would the next year anyway. But I was thirteen the year Uncle Gus forgot his mustache wax. He didn't notice until the next day, of course, but you woulda thought he forgot how to breathe. But that was a piss-poor example because Uncle Gus's lungs worked just fine based on all the commotion and yelling. This wasn't like forgetting a toothbrush or false teeth. This was like losing an arm.

He spent all day trying to fix the near sentient mustache, twirling it obsessively, using water and soap, even a hint of flour for a paste. "Serves him right," Aunt Linda muttered. She was enjoying the whole show. In the end, the left side looked like a sad, drooping rat's tail and the other side was a bird's nest of knots like it got tangled up trying to run away. The signature curve of the mustache was long gone.

Uncle Gus didn't want to go to the Good Friday evening service with us, I couldn't blame him. They were usually boring. Or maybe it was the fact that a couple of years ago one of the candles singed the edges of his mustache and lit up bright, the wax acting a lot like kerosine or something. Aunt Linda had taken much delight in being the one to throw her cup of coffee in his face under the pretense of putting out the flame. Apparently, he wasn't afraid of the sermon or catching on fire, he just couldn't manage to leave the house while engaged in an epic battle with the live creature on his face. "I just can't go," he muttered, looking sicker by the moment.

Aunt Linda opted to stay home with him, which was

quite a surprise considering she had knitted a new sweater for the event. It had bunnies and rather textured baby chickens and what Mom called "a gaudy display", a tinsel embroidered angel.

"In the fifty years I've lived with him, I've never seen him this upset," Aunt Linda said. This was a surprise considering we'd just celebrated their forty-fifth anniversary back in September.

Church was long and boring, as usual. There were extra hymns and only two people managed to light their sweaters on fire with the "blasted candle heathen experience" as Granny called it. But it was the best part of the whole service, sitting there with the candle in hand, watching the wax melt. We got home late because the Rev. just went on and on and so did the "halleluja-ers" too. We didn't see Uncle Gus or Aunt Linda but that wasn't much of a surprise. They were early risers and early bedders.

The next morning Mom and my other aunt, Louise, were busy making pancakes in the kitchen. Louise had brats for kids and Mom and Aunt Louise were busy scolding them for letting the chickens out and eating the whipped cream. I kept looking around for Uncle Gus or Aunt Linda, but they didn't show, which was weird 'cause they were usually the first ones up, making lots of coffee and noise.

We finally decided to sit down without them, leaving two places empty for when they decided to show. Dad was in the middle of a long-winded prayer he only used when other people were around when I heard their footsteps coming down the stairs. Then I heard a giggle. And then another. I looked up and found a stranger in the house! A bare-faced Uncle Gus. The only reminder of the mustache was a few scrapes on his upper lip, probably from having to wrestle that beast down in order to shave it clean off.

No one could think of anything to say. Aunt Linda smiled, which I think was the first time in her whole life she'd done that, and patted Uncle Gus on the arm, all sweet and nice. It was not like her usual smacks. Uncle Gus grinned back at her and said, "What a lovely morning!"

My dad smiled, muttering into his coffee, "Gus has risen, folks."

OUIJA BOARD

Penny spread the board out on the rickety, splintered attic floor. Despite the late hour and the darkness swirling about outside, it was stuffy and hot, like a piece of summer got stuck in between the rafters.

"You think it'll work?" Jonas asked.

Robin scoffed. She always did that. "Of course, it won't work. This is just a stupid game." She rubbed dust from her nose.

"But people have said they've *seen* things—said that it did things!" Jonas said, pointing at the board while being very cautious not to actually touch it.

Penny made sure the board was straight. She wasn't afraid to touch it, although she only used the tips of her fingers and the edges of the faded board to push it into place. "Yeah, but that could be part of the game." Penny laughed a wicked cackle. "Tell everyone you saw something to make the game scarier." She jabbed Jonas in the side, and he jumped.

Jonas looked down at the board and bit his lip. "But still, the stories had to start somewhere," he mumbled.

"Whatever," Robin said, crossing her arms over her chest, doing her best teacher impression. "Let's see for ourselves if it's true. Have you got the candles?"

Penny produced a few oblong and broken candles from her skirt pocket. She'd nicked them from church, but she figured it was best not to mention that, considering what they were about to do.

"Anything to light it with?" Robin asked. She was like the nanny of the group; she was only the oldest by two months, but she acted like she was like a mother hen. Penny suspected if she confessed her candle thievery, Robin might actually lay an egg.

"Didn't think that far, I guess," Jonas said.

"Doesn't matter," Penny said. "It's just for show." The single lightbulb illuminating the small attic space flickered.

Jonas swallowed hard. "Right."

Robin looked a little uncomfortable, but she tried to hide it by giving out orders. "Penny, grab the glass thingy. Jonas, double check the door."

Jonas groaned. "It's locked. No one comes up here, anyway."

They were hiding out in Jonas's Pop's attic above the wood shop. It was the best meeting place; they were far enough away from the main house that their inevitable outbursts wouldn't awaken their sleeping grandparents. Penny and Robin lived down the gravel road just a bit, and cutting through the field always shaved off ten minutes of walking time.

Penny wiggled her eyebrows. "Look what I snatched." She pulled a half-empty bottle from her bag. It was red, like blood, and she looked eager to dip into it.

"Where'd you get that!" Robin exclaimed, trying to hush herself. She didn't want to wake the dogs.

Penny shrugged. "The cellar at church. Swiped it last Sunday after Mama got stuck talking with Mrs. Candy." It was easier confessing this theft than the stupid candle snatching.

Robin and Jonas nodded. Talking with Mrs. Candy was like falling into a pit of honey—it was always hard to get out.

"What are we gonna do with it?" Jonas asked. He licked his chapped lips and flinched at the coyotes howling at the moon.

"We take a drink!" Penny popped the top off, took a giant swig, then spewed it all over the board. She coughed and hacked and shook out her tongue.

"Oh!" Robin exclaimed. "Ew, it's all over the board . . . Think that'll mess it up?"

"No," Penny said, wiping the sour wine from her chin away. "I think it'll only make it better."

"Should I take a drink?" Jonas asked.

"Only if you like the taste of roadkill." Penny shivered.

"Let's just start," Robin said, pushing the bottle away as if it were a dangerous thing.

"Right." Penny's face grew serious.

Jonas did his best not to look sick. "What do we do?"

"Put your hands on this piece." Penny tapped the little triangle with dirty glass for the center.

"Where did you find this anyway?" Robin asked.

"Garage sale," Penny said. "Mama wouldn't let me have it—said it was a heathen's thing, so I guess that means used ones still work. I went back later for it."

"Who are we gonna contact?" Jonas asked, his sweaty hand quivering as he touched the piece.

"Figured I'd call my Uncle Roy."

"Why him?" Robin asked.

Penny shrugged. "He's the worst person I know who is dead. Mama said he had a one-way ticket to hell since he died on his motorcycle from drinking too much."

"Why do you wanna talk to someone in hell?" Jonas asked, fighting the urge to rip his hand away from the corner of the piece.

"I just wanna see if it's real, you know?" Penny said. "Don't *you*? I mean, if I knew for sure hell was *real* I'd feel even worse about breaking Mama's vase and blaming the dog. I'd fess up to a lot more stuff, you know?"

Robin went from her summer sun complexation to a pale white. "I don't want it to be real."

Jonas swallowed hard. "But what if there's no answer? What if there's nothing after we die? Doesn't that seem just as scary?"

There was a long pause, the only sound the whistling and whimpering of the wind outside.

Penny cleared her throat. "Let's just try it and find out."

"What do we say?" Jonas asked.

"I think we start by asking Uncle Roy to come and join us."

"Like, his ghost?" Jonas snatched his hand away, but Penny pulled it back and forced it back onto the corner of the glass.

"No, I don't think so," Penny said. "He uses the board to talk to us—see the yes and no carving? He'll move the piece there if we ask him questions. And the alphabet, he can spell out answers too. We just have to keep our hands on the piece—that's what keeps us connected."

Robin swallowed hard, some color finally coming back to her cheeks. "Well, I guess we can start." She cleared her throat. "Penny's Uncle Roy? Are you there?"

The piece jiggled, but it didn't really move.

"Oh, Jonas, quit your quivering," Robin scolded.

"Wasn't me!" Jonas hissed.

"Uncle Roy? You there?" Penny whispered.

And the piece moved. It pulled their hands down and definitively over the *Yes* mark.

"He's here!" Jonas exclaimed.

"Yeah," Robin breathed.

"Uncle Roy?" Penny asked. "You in hell?"

The piece didn't move, it only remained hovering over the *Yes*.

"What's that mean?" Jonas asked. "I didn't feel it move . . . Is it a leftover *yes* or a real *yes*?"

"I dunno," Penny said. "I'll ask a *no* question. Uncle Roy, did you die in your sleep?"

The piece hummed and pulled the hands of the trio to the *No* square.

"Okay, I'll try again. Uncle Roy, are you in hell?"

The piece didn't move.

"Guess we don't really know," Robin said.

"Penny's Uncle Roy," Jonas said, getting new courage, "is it hot where you're at?"

Nothing.

"*Mmmkay*. Is it cold?" Jonas asked.

The piece moved, hovering over the *Yes*.

"Huh. I didn't really think heaven or hell was cold," Robin mused.

"Uncle Roy," Penny said, "where are you?"

"Penny!" Jonas hissed. "You asked the wrong kind of question." But even as he spoke, the little piece flew across the tattered board, smearing the drops of red wine like some sticky painting. The piece flew across the letters.

"A-L-O-N-E," Robin spelled aloud.

"Alone," Penny whispered. She bit her lip so had blood misxed with the wine staining her skin. "Uncle Roy, you think you could explain some more?"

The lack of movement made the kids stir; sweat dripped down their temples, tracing lines down their spines.

"Too big of a question, I think," Jonas said.

Penny nodded, gripping the corner of the piece fiercely. "I need another question."

"You could ask him what his favorite color is?" Jonas said.

"I already know that!" Penny hissed. "Why would I need to know that? I wanna know where he is, what happens after we die, you know?"

Robin nodded, biting her lip. She was always the

smartest, and Penny waited for her answer. "Ask him if he knows he's dead."

"Uncle Roy," Penny said, new confidence surging through her, "you know you're dead, right? Smacked right into a light pole. You know you didn't make it, right?"

The piece flew to the *Yes* space on the board.

"Well, at least we know he's still there," Jonas said. "Why are you so curious about what happens when we die?" Jonas was growing more irritable; the unknown and finally *knowing* it made him shiver and shake.

"Just want to," Penny said. "Uncle Roy, what's it like being dead?"

And the piece flew across the board. Penny read them aloud. "L-O-N-E-L-Y."

"Lonely," Robin whispered. She was always the best at reading.

Penny flipped up the board, scattering the glass piece and their hands.

"What the heck was that for?" Jonas asked, secretly relieved it was over.

"I'm done," Penny said. "I gotta go. Mama's gonna check my bed sometime, I know it."

Robin nodded, rubbing her hands like she was cold despite the suffocating heat of the cramped attic. "I should go too."

"All right," Jonas said, opening the hatch door and leading the descent. "What about the board? You can't just leave it here!"

"Throw it away or something," Penny said. "I'm done with it."

"I can't do that!" Jonas said. "Won't I be cursed or something?"

"Just throw it in the fireplace or burn pile. Or bury it in the woods," Penny said. She walked into the forest without a backward glance.

"What the heck was that about?" Jonas asked Robin.

"I don't know," Robin said. "Look, I'll take it and throw it in the river on my way home, that work?"

"I guess." Jonas wasn't convinced.

"See you at church," Robin said, sneaking out into the night.

Meanwhile, Penny was busy stomping her way through the forest. She slipped onto the porch but was discovered when the old, half-blind coonhound started to howl.

Mama shuffled down the stairs, headscarf covering her baldness. She looked thinner at night, like the darkness pulled more blood from her body. Maybe that's how blood moons got their red.

"Penny-Anne Louis Thompson, what the hell have you been up to?"

"Couldn't sleep." It wasn't a lie.

"Get your little pink butt in here before I decide to paddle it."

Penny stomped up the stairs and into the house, making a beeline to her room. She flopped on the bed, shut her eyes so tight the blackness turned blue and little spots danced around.

Mama coughed. Penny's eyes snapped open, and she jumped from her bed. She ambled over to Mama's room, where she sat up in bed, trying to drink water with shaking hands and a heaving chest.

"Am I keeping you up?"

"No," Penny said, walking over to hold the glass steady.

After Mama drank her fill, she leaned back on the several pillows. Penny jumped in bed too, curling up next to Mama, drifting to sleep to the rhythm of ragged breathing. Better to make sure Mama didn't have to spend life alone too.

ALL MOM'S FAULT

Mothers wear their lives on their skin. Worry lines from their baby's first solo drive. Burn marks on their chests from spilling hot coffee over themselves during their toddler's haphazard hug. The color in their hair sucked away in the hospital while worrying by their sick child's side. Mothers are marked and scarred.

But she started her life with scribbles and scrawls. The lines on her back a gift from her mother, and her cigarette burns a parting gift from her father. But she had my name tattooed on her lip, so she could taste me whenever she wanted. She had our first date written on her wrist, the start of us right there on her pulse. When she was forced to choose—"him or us"—she chose me. And her family screamed and cried. But they didn't carve tears on her face like she did.

She wrote "707" on her other wrist. Our first house. She created a log of firsts down her arm. *Job. Broken Leg.*

Wine. Freedom. Family. She tattooed the word "home" on her abdomen. She had many ideas, the best conceived was a girl named Piper. She tattooed songbirds on her throat because she sang a lot back then. A solo turned duet, Piper and her.

Then her home collapsed, and our house didn't feel the same. She scratched out the words "home" from her belly and replaced them with "Piper" and a date that was meaningless to others. It marked the end of the song, the duet was over. No encore here.

But she got tired of looking at that date and scratched it out again, covering it with big black letters: "ALL MOM'S FAULT."

She etched "do not touch" on her chest and scratched my name from her mouth. Barbed wire circled her arms, covering the garden of flowers she once had. Winter came and the color fled from her body. She boarded the door to her womb. Sealed off her heart.

Mothers had scars from growing their own families. Lines and battle wounds across their bellies. But some mothers are not mothers at all.

PAPER CRANES

He was sick. Not "the sniffles" sick. Not "surgery can fix this" sick. No, he was being eaten alive by little cancerous cells. She'd witnessed her husband's life and body be consumed by the microscopic devils for the last year, and all the while, she'd had to just sit and watch. That felt like the worst punishment of all.

Those little devils were working away at his bones, lungs, and other vital organs as he sat staring blankly at the telly. Despite his still body and eyes, his hands never paused. They worked with practiced rhythm, like a dance with his fingers. Folding those paper cranes. Those *damned* paper cranes.

She sat in her chair, staring at his hands and his vacant eyes. She had a gaze that could make a cactus wither, and she imagined that she could stare beyond his skin and make those cancer cells shrivel under her harsh glare. She'd been trying for the last year. It hadn't worked. So now, she glared at God, hoping that was enough to make the deity who was supposed to be on her side wither away. Or maybe her stare would force God into action and he would finally smite those blasted cells like she'd been praying for. It didn't work. She was tired of glaring. She was tired of praying. Pleading.

He held up a finished product. "Like this one? It's green—your favorite shade too." It was, and despite her earlier glaring concentration, she cracked a smile. And he did too. But the effort exhausted him, and he went back to folding cranes. He talked while he folded. "Remember the first one I made you?"

She laughed and that barest flash of a memory made her feel normal for a moment. "That spaghetti-stained napkin you somehow managed to fold into a crane? Yeah, I do." She laughed again and hoped it might have scared those cancer cells away. "You left it on my car. Lucky it didn't rain."

"Lucky you unfolded it."

She nodded. "Lucky I took a chance and called you. No, the luckiest thing was that I was able to read that chicken scratch you call handwriting."

He smiled again, his hands still folding another square of paper. It wasn't his real smile. His real smile was crooked and revealed his lower snaggle tooth. This smile was straight and not wide enough to show the real him.

"What do I have to do?" she whispered.

"Do?" he whispered back.

"How do I fix it? How do you go to sleep at night

knowing you might not wake up? Why don't you fight it, stay awake? Don't give it a chance to take you away."

He held up a crane. "I am a bird. Time for me to fly home."

She didn't push for him to say more, she never did.

And she didn't know why he folded the cranes; it was always his strange habit. He'd always needed something to do with his hands—while at the doctor's office, or while waiting in line, and heck, even at Christmas dinner. He'd use receipts, napkins, even dollar bills to fold his little cranes. And he folded more cranes until he went into his room. Those cancer cells took that connection from them too. He coughed and moaned with every movement. The guilt he carried for keeping her awake was worse. So they slept apart, trying to maintain their original connection despite living like roommates.

He talked to God like a friend he was excited to see. She screamed at God for stealing him away. She mumbled "thief" and "murderer" under her breath, giving God the finger whenever her husband groaned in pain.

Months or weeks had passed. She'd gone from counting every day to trying to forget them altogether. It was hard to tell when every evening was the same. Until it wasn't. Until his hands stopped moving and he didn't shuffle off to his room. The paper crane he had been working on slipped from his too-still hands and fell to the floor. An orange one. It was like the last leaf of autumn, announcing the dark arrival of winter.

Grief was cold. It slipped its way deep into her bones and froze her from the inside out. Grief was a ghost that hovered behind her, waiting to wrap its icy arms around her when she got too close to the past, got too close to him. Grief was a gray fog.

When the funeral flowers wilted and dried, she still found those cranes. Green ones, pink ones, orange and yellow ones, too. She had expected to find them, expected boxes in his sick room, but she didn't. Instead, she found them in all the places she shouldn't.

The first time, her stomach dropped. He used to write notes on the cranes he'd leave on the coffee pot, in her lunches. But to open her glovebox and find one waiting for her? It was like a kiss on the cheek from a friendly ghost.

She thought it had been luck. But when she lifted a can of chicken noodle soup from the pantry, an involuntary tear sprang up when, underneath the last soup can, she discovered another crane. A pink one.

His notes were concise and sweet, just like his life had been.

Hey baby,

I love your smile, and the way you bite your lip when you are just about to throw your knitting project down and vow never to try that confounded hobby again, just to pick it up and try again the next day. I'll miss that.

They were scattered all over. She was nearly afraid to do a deep clean of their small home, for fear of finding them all. For fear of the day they'd run out, the day she'd lose him all over again. But even after she worked up the courage—and found thirteen new cranes in the process —she still managed to find more.

He had actually stuffed one behind her fake orchid.

Hey baby,

Finally gonna graduate to a real plant? I vote for a cactus.

It was when she was cleaning out the boxes in the garage (looking for a pot for the new cactus) that she found another.

Hey baby,

I have a confession. You always thought I was a boob guy, and I was, until I met your ass.

She couldn't help but take a peek at her buttocks. It wasn't nearly as nice as before. It had been just over a year since they'd buried him, and she hadn't gone on one run since. They used to ride bikes too. Like kids, chasing each other through the streets on their second-hand bikes they found at a thrift store. She found the next one under the bike pump.

Hey baby,

Remember that bike ride we took in Colorado? We were grossly under-prepared, but it was one of the best trips we ever had. Though I don't think my tailbone ever recovered.

She found another under the bird seed out in the garage when she finally thought it was time to give those blue jays some love.

Hey baby,

I said I was a bird. They don't know when to fly home. They don't know why they are called to return to the place of their birth. But they go. It was the same for me; I think. And I'm sad it was early. But I'm home.

He always was the ever faithful one. Taking things in stride. She was the one who needed answers. Demanded them from the creator, resented God when he was silent. *Home* was a foreign concept now.

But life moved on. Eventually the trees gained color. Orange leaves still reminded her of funerals. Grief was still a shadow. It always would be. Sometimes it was a giant black mist, trying to suffocate her. Sometimes it sat quiet, hidden in a corner.

And these things went on. And she got back to the life she used to live with him. But it was like trying to function with only one arm or leg. She felt his absence, but life wouldn't stop.

She went from glaring and berating God to simply arguing with him. She talked loud and often, anything to keep grief small and in the corner. Sometimes she screamed at God for making her husband a bird and taking him home too soon.

And years later she thought the cranes were all gone, but she found one randomly stuck in a book she finally got around to reading. Psalms seemed like a good place to start. Everyone liked Psalms. But when she opened to the middle, she couldn't help but notice a lump in the pages and flipped forward a few books to Jeremiah. *Jeremiah?*

"Even the stork in the sky knows its seasons, and the dove, the swallow, and the crane observe the time for migration. But my people don't know the requirements of the Lord." Jeremiah 8:7

She smoothed out the crane.

Hey Baby,

Glad you made it back here.

THE INHERITANCE

"That thing will do anything you need out in the field. It's sharp and sturdy, can cut through most bone, and can be delicate enough to skin the animal if you're clever enough with your fingers."

The hunting knife was heavy in my hands. I thought I could see dried blood in the grooves. The handle was smooth from years of use, and I couldn't wait until my hand was big enough to lift it easily.

My dad took it back and turned it in his hand before taking it to the stone and sharpening it. "My own dad, your grandpa, left it for me. Sort of. He used it to slit his wrists. He walked out to the river and sat on the banks. When I found him, he was splayed out, like he changed his mind when he was half empty." Dad's face went still. "It was like a bloody angel; the red was so bright against the snow. He'd been there so long, he'd frozen to the ground."

I wiped my hands on my jeans, wanting to get whatever might be left on the knife off of my skin.

Dad went back to sharpening. "But I got to keep this knife, though; it's done this family well, all things considered. Used to be my own Grandpappy's."

Dad took to looking out the window after that. Gazing into the woods, searching for something. I'd pull him away sometimes, asking to play cards, go out fishing, maybe eat dinner. He grew thin like the trees when they lost their leaves.

He and I walked to the bridge that crossed the river. It was early in the morning; the cold bit at our faces. We didn't say anything when he dropped the hunting knife over the ledge. It didn't make much of a splash, and I wondered if the river managed to gobble it up and pull it downstream before it sunk to the bottom. Maybe in summer, when the water slowed and the river all but dried up, we could know for sure.

But come spring, Dad walked back to the spot where he tossed the knife. He made a habit of staring at the river, like he was looking for that knife. He jumped off that bridge before summer came, when the water was still high. They found him not a mile away, washed up on shore, arms splayed like some starfish that managed to get lost in freshwater. The river spit him out.

I didn't think about that knife much. I tried not to think about bloody snow angels, freshwater starfish, or my dad. But at every river I was near, I just had to pause and check. I had to scan the shore, and if the water was clear, search the bottom, because maybe the hunter's knife was there. Maybe it made it all the way across state lines. Maybe it was jostled and churned right out into the ocean.

I finally made it there, to the sea, years later. I was not really happy, nor sad. A strange emptiness left me hollow, like my blood was really water; the years of staring at the rivers made a scar on my heart. And walking into that great big body of blue didn't help me find it, either. Somewhere out there is a knife no one will remember.

SHE'S A THIEF

First, she stole my energy. Walking was a challenge. Everything hurt, and I was out of breath. She stole the oxygen from my lungs, if I was able to get any at all.

Next, Cancer stole my hair. That was fine. What was hair to me, anyway? It was gray and frayed and at the end of its life, anyhow. Nothing special to me.

Then Cancer stole my family. Sort of. It was a byproduct of the medication, so I can still blame her. My visits with the grandbabies were cut short because I was tired, or they were sick. No more school plays and piano recitals for me.

Cancer stole my family's happiness. Cancer painted clown faces over their sad mouths and eyes. I could scrub away the fake smiles and happy lips, but I couldn't seem to wash away those sad smiles and teary eyes.

Cancer stole my savings. It was only money. That was fine. But it's worth mentioning that Cancer is a thief.

Cancer stole my eyebrows. And that probably hurt the worst. Those two lines above my eyes could explain more than any smile or frown could. I could make my dog come to heel at my side with the twitch of an eyebrow. I could make the grandbabies mind with a simple arch of my left brow. Not anymore. My brows became a blank canvas. Unexpressive and boring. Cancer stole the power I wielded in the form of eyebrows.

"It's not that big of a deal," my son said, laughing as I complained.

"It is." I gave him a scowl, one that should have made him shake in his boots. That ugly-mom-face every mother developed when their child turned two. He didn't even flinch. *Damn these bald brows.*

"Just draw them on, or tattoo them." He laughed again, unable to see the severity of the situation. I could have made him eat that laugh and choke on his hasty apology if I still had my eyebrows.

I learned on the YouTube how to even them out with a special pencil. I repeated to myself, "sisters, not twins." Eventually, I was satisfied. They almost looked like my old ones. I gave them a wiggle and they looked almost like the real deal in the mirror.

Despite the early morning and the dim house, I walked down the hall and into the kitchen. I glanced at the steps leading upstairs to what was once my room. I had to move to the first floor when the stairs turned into a mountain I just couldn't summit. That was another thing Cancer took—my balance and stairs.

I made eggs and toast and set to work getting out

the dishes and pancake stuff. Sundays were brunch days. Cancer hadn't had a chance to take that yet. She still tried, and sometimes it was all I could do to keep her filthy hands out of my pancake Sundays, but I managed.

The kids would be over, and we'd eat pancakes with too much syrup and strawberries, and I'd watch the grandkids wrestle in the yard. My time in the hospital took that from me, but I got it back, fought and clawed for it. I'm the one who taught the kiddos to wrestle, anyhow.

Just as the orange juice was placed on the big table, a knock sounded and the door burst open, followed by a flood of flailing arms and legs. My four grandbabies ran in for hugs. I didn't even wince when they wrapped their arms around me. I mastered schooling my features, and they couldn't even see how much my body was bruised at their affection.

"Hey, Mom," my eldest son said, giving me a much gentler hug.

"Hi, Mom." My youngest did the same, and we all sat down to eat, their spouses trying to corral their kids while my own corralled my medications and made note of what they needed to refill and pick up this week.

I gave each grandkid an extra dollop of whipped cream on their pancakes, and it was our little secret. They giggled and laughed and whispered to one another all through breakfast and I was able to use my ugly-grandma-face (and new eyebrows) to get them in line. As soon as their plates were cleared, they ran out into the backyard, ready to play in the giant sandpit I would never cover. I'd laid all their buckets and shovels out that morning for them, too.

I stood, slowly, trying to push the pain from my back away.

"Sit, Mom," my daughter said. "David and I want to talk to you."

I was suddenly glad for the eyebrows. They were like war paint, and I was ready for whatever nonsense my own kiddos were about to unleash. Their spouses left with "good luck" written all over their faces, heading out back to watch the kids play and yell at them for throwing sand at each other.

"Mom," David started, "I don't think you can keep doing this. We need to talk about more long-term care."

"No," I said.

"This can't go on. You are exhausted all the time. You need help. Maybe you can go—"

"*No.*" I furrowed my brows and squared him off. "I'll hire someone, but I won't leave my home. I won't leave this." I pointed to the wide-open back door, the singsong voices of my grandkids floating in.

My son looked relieved. My daughter nodded. "Honestly, that was a lot easier than we thought."

"What?" I asked. I hadn't expected to win so easily. I regretted not using that eyebrow pencil thing sooner. Sure, it took time, maybe there was a stencil or something to make it easier.

My son laughed. "You are hiring help. We thought it would be like pulling teeth to get that from you."

I shrugged, and even that hurt. "Cancer has taken a

lot from me, but I can age with dignity. At least I can still wipe my own ass."

They laughed at that. "Now . . ." My son grew serious again, while my daughter stared at my eyebrows. "I have to ask you something."

I nodded, giving him my best I-am-your-mother-and-I-will-listen-to-whatever-you-have-to-say-even-if-you-did-something-terrible face.

He stifled a laugh, and I was offended. My expression was serious, no nonsense.

His mouth broke into a grin. "What the hell is with the eyebrows?"

My daughter held up a little makeup mirror. I was faced with my penciled-on eyebrows. They were brown, which I admit in this light didn't match my skin tone particularly well. But beyond that, they were smudged and sparkly. *Sparkled eyebrow pencil.* Who would create such a product?

My daughter snorted; my son was red-faced and cackling. I now knew why the kiddos were whispering at breakfast. And that's how Cancer stole my vanity.

CLAM CHOWDER

She always loved a classic black shoe. So when she walked out of their room wearing her favorite ones (the laces on the left, Velcro on the right), Jerry just hoped it was because she couldn't decide which pair to wear. But he knew that wasn't true.

"Ready to go?" he asked, standing from his recliner, and reaching for his hat and coat draped over the old piano. It was the new drop-off spot for keys, change, coats, and gloves.

"Go where?" she asked.

"To lunch. It's Friday."

"Oh, yes." Perdy smiled. "Clam chowder?"

"Yep. Clam chowder Fridays." Their weekly ritual was unbroken, save by the occasional vacation and sick day (and even then, they'd simply bring the chowder back to the house). They had been getting cozied up and walking down the long street to the little hole-in-the-wall diner since they moved into the place forty-some-odd years ago. He chose to ignore the fact that she *always* asked if it was clam chowder day. He also chose to ignore that he was ignoring her worsening state—a strange yearning to forget about everything and live in her own little world.

This Friday was no different. He opted not to mention the mismatched shoes and helped her get into her coat. She held his hand tight as they walked the sidewalk and for a moment, for a few strides, it felt like he was twenty again. He almost wished he had helped her put on her signature red lipstick, but she had been in a good mood and eager to go, so he jumped at the easy time it was to get her out of the house. It was growing increasingly difficult. Sometimes he could bribe her with the prospect of going out for ice cream, sometimes just mentioning a walk in the park was enough to get her out of a downward spiral the walls of their home could bring on.

Her mind was slipping away, and he thought being surrounded by evidence of their favorite memories together—the photos, the piano—might stave off the anxieties of not remembering them reliably. Maybe spark a flame that would burn away the disease. But it didn't. When she saw a face in a photograph that had been hanging on their wall for years and couldn't recognize the faces, she grew angry. She knew she should remember, and she knew she was forgetting.

But she still remembered him.

The bell chimed when they walked through the familiar doors.

"Howdy, folks!" Mary called out. "Coffee today?"

"Yes," Perdy said.

Normally she was hesitant, looking to him to answer, and this glimpse of her old self made Jerry smile. "Two, please."

They took their seats at the usual booth. Jerry couldn't help but think the worn and torn cushions were mostly their fault. This was *their* booth.

"Hey, Jerry," Mary whispered. "I hate to do this, but we are out of clam chowder."

Jerry's stomach tightened. He bit his lip so hard, he tasted warm blood. She had remembered this. Perdy *knew* about this. This was part of their routine. Would this unravel the months they took creating a life she could participate in through muscle memory?

"That's okay," he whispered. *No, it wasn't.* Perdy was busy reading the menu. "What else ya got?"

"The only other soup is chicken noodle."

"All right," he said. "Two of those, please, and—"

"Extra crackers." Mary winked.

"Thank ya, hon."

Moments later, Mary returned with two large bowls full of piping hot chicken noodle soup. It smelled delightful and his stomach growled. Mary returned only a moment later with a basket of their favorite crackers.

"I think I ordered the other soup," Perdy said.

"They were out of that, love," Jerry said. It was like he was parenting all over again, hoping this major change did not create a scene or tantrum.

"I wanted the other soup. The chowder." Perdy dropped the spoon and tore into a cracker packet with shaking hands, cramming them in her face. "I'll eat these, you eat that." She pointed to the soup.

"No love, Mary made this special for us."

"Mary was never nice to me."

Jerry stole a glance at the waitress—thankfully, she seemed not to hear. He lowered his voice. "Perdy, she has always been our waitress, and she likes you. She made you cookies, remember?" *Of course, she didn't.*

He wanted to bite his tongue after that. Asking someone who lost their memories to *remember* wasn't a physical act, like opening a jar. You didn't just twist harder and hope the lid popped off. It was unfair. It was like asking someone to describe a brand-new color.

"I think we should go," she said.

Despite her age, Perdy could power walk like she was a child. She was out of the diner before Jerry had time to drop some bills on the table. He was only able to scoop up their coats and chase after her when Mary hollered, "Just go, Jerry! We'll see ya later." The waitress gave him a small nod, twisting her hands in front of her. She'd known Perdy back when she was whole.

He managed to catch her and wrap her up in the fluffy coat she had always loved and guide her back home. She was agitated, her voice shaking. She was hungry, and that low blood sugar did nothing to calm her.

"We got some cans of clam chowder in the pantry," he said. "I'll heat some up real fast when we get back home." This was his time to shine, and he only hoped his weak wrists would be able to turn the can opener fast enough.

She nodded and they walked in silence. When they entered their little house, he got her settled on the couch while he bustled in the kitchen, looking for the cans he knew were there. He had them heating on the stove when music floated into his ears.

The dusty piano sang a lively tune. It was quiet at first, but then it reached a crescendo, the tempo racing along by the time he peeked around the corner.

Perdy sat upright, her hands flying across the keys. *Roll Out the Barrel* flew from her fingertips. She used to play for him all the time. He loved slow Jazz, while she loved the old show tunes and polka. No one liked polka —but there he was, standing in rapt fascination and actually *enjoying* it.

She hadn't played in years. He was afraid to prompt her to sit on the piano bench—afraid she would be met with that familiar feeling of knowing she should remember, knowing she was connected to the music, but not being able to reach out and actually find that connection.

When she finished, she gave him a giant smile. "I love that song."

"Me too," he said and was surprised to find himself being earnest. It was never easy to lie to her, even now.

"I'm hungry."

"Me too. Come sit—the soup is almost hot."

She sat in her usual spot, the months of routine finally becoming muscle memory. He set the piping hot bowl of clam chowder in front of her.

"Oh," she said, stirring it with the spoon, "I was hoping for some chicken noodle today."

Roll Out The Barrell
CLAMCHOWDER

ADENIUM OBESUM

He looked like he was ripped from an old picture book. He was wrinkled, worn at the edges. His voice was faded, his skin discolored from years in the sun. He didn't have friends, but he had the television and his Adenium Obesum. The television kept him company and the Desert Rose was pretty to look at. It sat in the terracotta pot on his coffee table, where it got the perfect amount of sun—and he was pretty sure it liked the sound of the morning news and jeopardy.

She would be blooming soon. The flowers would last about seven days. They'd be *perfect* for five. He had it marked on his calendar; these plants were so easy to schedule. He had a cactus out in the sunroom, ready to bloom in about a month. The African Violets, resting under the UV lights bloomed all year. He had a special long spoon used to feed the stems in the hard-to-reach places.

He worked as a paper pusher at the post office. Too old and tired to stand on his feet for such long hours, but not old enough to retire. Two more years, though. He was left to his own in the corner of the big square building. Sometimes he'd get a papercut and it would jolt him awake. He went days without a conversation. He'd say good morning, but he'd get no response. He even brought young Andy a coffee. The expensive and sugary kind. It sat at the counter all day, untouched.

After work, on his way to the grocery store, he stopped for gas. He only carried cash and had to nearly scream at the attendant inside, "Twenty-five on twelve!"

The attendant wouldn't look at him in the eye and never gave him a receipt. So, he went and filled his tank; it wasn't worth another attempt to get her attention. He just left the cash on the counter.

He went to the grocery store. He got a little turned around and asked an employee where the mustard was. She walked right by. Eventually he found another employee, a boy stocking the shelves.

"Excuse me, but do you know what isle the mustard is on?"

The boy said nothing. He finished with the rice and moved on to the beans.

And then the man knew what he had long been suspecting to be true. So, he took his basket of bacon and can of olives (a special treat) through the front door. No one came for him. No alarms sounded. No one noticed. He made it all the way to his car before he decided to turn around. The piece of brisket and aged gouda was just too tempting. He placed them in his basket and put the can of olives back, going for the kalamata ones instead. Even some garlic-stuffed ones. He grabbed dill Havarti too. And a bottle of sauce. The expensive kind. He found a fresh baguette too. And a rack of lamb. He looked at his goods, realizing he didn't have a cutting board big enough. So, he went to the small kitchen center and picked up the biggest one he could find. A knew knife and a cheese slicer too. And he walked out the front just the same as he entered, and no one looked at him.

He stopped by another store on his way home, picking up some charcoal and a new grill. It was tough getting it in his car with his old hands. He contemplated asking for help loading it up, but he knew it would have been pointless shouting on his part. He set up the new grill on the deck and filled it with fancy charcoal, mouth watering at the thought of brisket. He'd try the tri-tip next. Maybe even a pork loin.

The smoke billowed in the air and he wondered if people could see it. Or maybe the smoke was an extension of himself and invisible to the rest of the world.

The new knife cut it like butter. The cheese and olives were divine. He arranged his plate nicely, talking to the Desert Rose all the while. And when it was a feast fit enough for twelve, he dug in. The meats tasted delicious. The new knife cut it like butter. The cheese and olives were divine. A fraction was consumed when he decided it was time to share this board of food and his new gift.

He went out shopping a few more times. All new kitchen pots and pans. New towels too. The real treat were the new sheets—five thousand thread count. He had no idea they came with that many. He got things for his plants. A new pot for the monstera that never stopped growing. A fancy ceramic one. It was too heavy to lift into the back of the car, so he grabbed a new hand truck and wheeled it home. He got some fancy soil too and that lemon tree he'd been interested in trying to cultivate. It was sitting on his deck and she waved to him when he walked by now. She sat in a large pot so he could move the lemon tree inside when it got cold.

It was two days later when the ad he posted on Craigslist came through. He had used a simple line: "Widower Seeks Friend."

He received two pictures of penises. Neither interesting enough to follow up on, mostly because they didn't include any message. He received a note from a man in a wheelchair, and they chatted over email, but the wheelchair man stopped replying when the man mentioned liking shopping and cooking. But he also got a message from a woman. She'd been alone close to a decade too. She didn't have any plants, but seemed interested in learning about them.

He grabbed a few easy plants for her next time he went shopping. A ZZ plant and pothos vine. They were very hard to mess up. He practiced saying hello and using his voice. It had been so long. He talked to the plants and they listened and encouraged him. He gathered the new plants in his arms and walked to the coffee shop. But she wasn't there. Or maybe she was and she had gone invisible too.

He sat at the coffee shop for a long while, staring at

the patrons walking in and out, looking for a woman about his age who said she'd be wearing a red scarf. He left cradling the plants when the staff turned off the lights for the night.

He tucked the ZZ and pothos into their beds, setting them in the kitchen window so they could keep an eye on the persnickety lemon tree.

The Desert Rose was supposed to bloom. And the man had thought that maybe it was shy because it was late. Or even worse, maybe it only bloomed when it had an audience. But she eked out a few flowers and with some coaxing she stood tall in her pot, proudly displaying the pink flowers. The ZZ and pothos cheered from their perch in the kitchen. He even brought the lemon tree inside so she could marvel at the pink.

He continued to shop for meats and cheeses and plants. His small house became a jungle and he became thinner. Like the pages in an old book, he began to crack at the spine and pages began to slip away. And when the plants stopped recognizing him he knew he was truly faded, and like the paper of a book, he disintegrated with time, turning to compost to feed the flowers.

THE ORCHARD

I had my first cup of whiskey when I was nine. It was after Ma beat my backside so black and blue, Pa had handed me a flask full of the stuff. He said it'd help the pain. It burned my throat raw, but I drank it until I floated away. I used my pennies and nickels to buy the stuff. They all knew Ma in town; I told folks it was for her, but I kept it hidden in the orchards and would drink myself to the sky each night. Then it was gin, then it was vodka. Now I was thirty-two and my liver was black—just as black and blue as my backside the day it all started.

I hadn't been back to the orchards since I was fifteen. I left without a backward glance and worked to feed myself ever since. But I had Pony to worry about—this ugly mutt I picked up on the side of the road. He growled and barked and kept to himself mostly. Maybe that's why I stopped for him. I had been just the same when a stranger took a chance and picked me up. But old Pony had a few good years left in him, which was more than the doc said I'd get. So, we took a little trip.

We crossed the plains of Oklahoma in that truck I'd picked him up in. Stopped and camped under the stars in Kansas. Ate our fill of grits in Louisiana. Howled country songs all the way through Mississippi. I ignored the growing pain in my gut, the constant fatigue, and the yellow sheen of my skin. I was almost as yellow as the inside of the peaches scattering the ground of that damned orchard. They smelled just the same as I remembered. I hadn't had a peach in twenty years.

When I drove down that long, gravel driveway, I recalled my summers getting lost in the maze of those winding trees. Ma loved those trees more than she loved me, and I had to take a chance on her loving Pony a little more than me, too. I rolled to a stop and opened the passenger door. I needed a minute to catch my breath, but I managed to push old Pony out and closed the door just in time. I drove away from that farm for the second time, still refusing to look back.

BLUEBERRY PIES

"I still don't know how you manage to keep that bush alive," my mother said, pinching down the sides of the pie crust. The edges were scalloped, like her apron.

I shrugged. "It just grows and grows."

And we made pie when it exploded with fruit. When June rolled around, and the plant hunched with the weight of the berries, we took up the same posture, bending over the bush, picking buckets of them, then bowed in supplication over the table, making three dozen pies or so. They froze nicely. The crispy top didn't look as nice when they came out of the freezer, but the tart and sweet combination of the fresh berries managed to taste exactly the same. Plus, pies were better than jam any day.

"She don't like to take care of the outside stuff," Tim said, popping a beer open and stealing a handful of berries off the table.

"You ought to take care of it." My mother pointed a gooey spatula at me. "It's not like you to let things go like that," my mother said again, wiping the flour from her hands and plucking a rogue berry from the table, popping it into her mouth. The dark purple stained her teeth like blood. "Now pinch it down better, hon. Pinch it like this so they don't all come out looking crooked."

Mama died that spring, and the bush followed along with her. It was a sign. I cried when I dug up the dry and dead bush—a reverse burial of sorts. I winced when I shoved it in the debris bin. Tim punched it down. I flinched when the lid snapped shut.

Then I buried myself under blankets, suffocating in darkness. The dark was tart, like a young blueberry. It was sharp like Mama's strong fingers. I wanted to use that pointed darkness and shove that tartness into my veins. Have a piece of Mama with me or something. Instead, I buried another layer of blankets over me. And then another. Maybe I was buried deeper than the roots of that stupid blueberry bush were. Maybe I'd be lucky and never get out.

"Alright, enough—" I was hauled out from under my makeshift grave by Tim. "You got to get yourself in order."

He hauled me into the car, gripping my arm so tightly that when he finally let go, little blue dots sprouted on my pale arms. Like blueberries. "You're gonna go see Dr. Pike."

Tim was smart, said he had a head full of brains and I believed him. He said I could stop seeing the therapist if he decided that the doctor was a schmuck. I simply stared at the blueberry bruises on my arm.

I'd pictured Dr. Pike to be this squat man with a large mouth, like the fish. Instead, he was a she. And she was tall, like an asparagus stalk. With a hairdo to match.

There wasn't one of those fancy couches to lay on either. Just two chairs pointing at each other, a desk along the wall, and the asparagus.

"Let's just get to know each other," Dr. Pike said. "See what's going on."

I nodded. "Do you like blueberries?"

She nodded. "I do. One of my favorites, actually. Do you?"

"They remind me of my mother."

"That's not really an answer to my question," the doctor said.

And I saw Dr. Pike again. It took only fourteen more sessions for me to realize that Tim's head was not full of brains. Just bad ideas and hot air. Another four sessions to realize that I could have ideas too.

It took a full year to realize that my mother's love wasn't really a mother's love. It was weak. Rotted. Failing at the roots and covered up with pretty words. Like that blueberry bush.

"Is it okay?" I asked the doctor. "Is it okay to miss her?"

"Of course," she said.

"Is it okay to mourn her even though I realize I don't like her? Didn't like her?"

"Grief is funny that way. I think that's more than okay."

"How do I refer to her? Is she then or now? She was but still is."

The asparagus only nodded slowly. There were no words. And yet there were so many.

"Time to fill in the holes," I said. It was that broken an empty spot in the yard. The empty hole where that blueberry bush once thrived. So I planted raspberries. It would be a year before they bloomed. But I think I liked those better, and they filled the space nicely. And I'd take care of the bush. The root would be strong. New pies would be made.

So I started making pies again. It was hard to make the crusts without Mama's scalloped apron to look at.

She was a pattern I'd followed. But I supposed a ruffled edge might do better now.

And when the pie was cooled and sitting on the table, I realized it was perfect. The best pie I'd ever made even though I'd forgone the scalloped crust and it was made out of raspberries. But it was still perfect. So I stuck my fist in it. Right in the middle I smashed my hand through the crust so hard the red filling exploded, splattering against my apron and skin.

I brought my hand to my lips, watching the red raspberries run down my hand like blood. I licked it up. It was bitter, and then it was sweet.

UNRAVEL

It was made up of all the colors of the rainbow. No, perhaps even *more* colors than the rainbow. The knitted afghan had every shade of blue, red, purple, pink, even yellow—and no one liked yellow. It was Gran's blanket, and it always sat above her favorite chair. It was thick and warm and smelled like Earl Grey tea and honey. Like her. And it still sat on her chair, even though she was gone.

Ellie said Gran should be buried in it. It would keep her warm and give her something to look at while she did whatever dead people stuck in boxes did. She could spend her time mending it, like she had done on so many nights. Or maybe adding a new row of color. It looked like it needed more green, anyway. She could fix the hole or fraying edges. Instead, the afghan sat where Gran should've been, looking equally as uncomfortable as Ellie did when she had to stare at it.

It used to be a game; she and Gran would talk about their favorite colors, each deciding which one they loved the most that day, since they loved all the colors so much. The rainbow looked gray now.

The afghan wandered the house at night. At first it was all the time, sliding from its spot on the chair, looking for Gran. It made it up the stairs and settled on Gran's bed. Ellie threw it back over the chair when she found it. She felt a little guilty, so she spoke gently to the blanket. "Gran is gone. Stay put now."

But the afghan didn't stay put. It sat at Gran's second favorite place, the porch swing. It soaked up the moonlight, growing dirty and ragged from the nightly ventures, picking up dust and dirt.

Ellie put it back on the chair. "She's not coming back." She said it a little harsher this time. The blanket was filthy after crawling over the dust bunnies. Ellie shook it out and couldn't decide if she was relieved or sad to find the ends were coming loose. The afghan was unraveling; the last color Gran added was a bright blue.

The next time she found the blanket in the garden, near the tomatoes. "She's not here. Go back to your spot!" The afghan didn't move, so Ellie gathered it up in her arms and threw it over the back of the chair once again.

The loose ends were getting worse. The hole was getting bigger. So Ellie picked at the ends, pulling the stitches loose. The bright blue yarn fell away easily. The next color was a dark blue. Ellie pulled at that too, all the way to the purple. Then red, then pink, then yellow, orange, green—everything. There was nothing left of that giant blanket but a pile of rainbow on the floor.

And, after a moment, she found herself putting it back together again.

ACKNOWLEDGMENTS

I must thank my husband, Malachi, first. Despite not being a reader and most of the time having NO clue what I am writing, you are always the most excited for me. Thank you! (Also, thank you for learning how to make THE BEST whiskey sours. They really did make this whole process more enjoyable.)

Thanks to my early beta reader, Victoria Wren! You were (like always) spot on with your critiques. It is an honor having you in my little writing corner.

Thank you to my second wave of beta readers, Victoria Wren (again), Adrian Santiago, Hannah R. Palmer, and Sue Olsen!

Also, thank you to Mattie Victoria for her wonderful illustrations! I shouted into the void, asking for help, and she answered!

This is a book that I worked on in solitude, mostly because I didn't know if it would work, and if this blend of happy and sad and real and raw and weird and strange would come together at all. But I think it did, so thank you, dear reader, for making it to the end of this little book!

Bethany Votaw gives you sixteen short stories featuring the darkness and the monsters surrounding us. Experience the uncomfortable realities lurking beneath the surface. Meet a devil at a coffee shop, discover what the Nightman is really after, and stumble upon strange creatures and events lurking just beneath the surface. If you like supernatural horror, psychological thrills, and mind-bending twists, then you'll love this debut short story collection by Bethany Votaw. Unlock *Scribbles and Scrawls* and begin the journey into madness.

Detective Adam Reis has everything to prove and mistakes to fix. He enlists the help of local search and rescue and an unlikely tracker to help him find a murderer who fled into the winter Montana wilderness. An old recluse, Clay, comes out of the forest when asked to be a tracker. Clay has his own secrets

to hide but reluctantly agrees to
help the young detective. Will these two unlikely men work
together to track a dangerous man through the fierce terrain
and snow? Or will their own secrets be their downfall? Find
out in Tracker.

ABOUT THE AUTHOR

Bethany Votaw started writing in college on little note cards in an effort to stay awake during chemistry. If you can't find her, she is probably taking a nap on the beach or playing in a river.

Feel free to follow her on Instagram @bethanyjvotaw (where she tries to post regularly) or on Twitter @bethanyvotaw (where she posts nonsense) or sign up for her newsletter at www.bethanyjvotaw.com (where she sometimes, on the rare occasion when she has her act together, sends important monthly updates and secret stories).

COPYRIGHT